DETROIT PUBLIC LIBRARY
3 5674 05610046 5

P9-EMH-420

CARTEL PUBLICATIONS
PRESENTS
NEFARIOUS
T. STYLES
NATIONAL BEST SELLING AUTHOR OF *RAUNCHY*

ARE YOU ON OUR EMAIL LIST?

SIGN UP ON OUR WEBSITE

www.thecartelpublications.com

OR TEXT THE WORD:

CARTELBOOKS TO 22828

FOR PRIZES, CONTESTS, ETC.

CHECK OUT OTHER TITLES BY THE CARTEL PUBLICATIONS

SHYT LIST 1: BE CAREFUL WHO YOU CROSS

SHYT LIST 2: LOOSE CANNON

SHYT LIST 3: AND A CHILD SHALL LEAVE THEM

SHYT LIST 4: CHILDREN OF THE WRONGED

SHYT LIST 5: SMOKIN' CRAZIES THE FINALE'

PITBULLS IN A SKIRT 1

PITBULLS IN A SKIRT 2

PITBULLS IN A SKIRT 3: THE RISE OF LIL C

PITBULLS IN A SKIRT 4: KILLER KLAN

POISON 1

POISON 2

VICTORIA'S SECRET

HELL RAZOR HONEYS 1

HELL RAZOR HONEYS 2

BLACK AND UGLY

BLACK AND UGLY AS EVER

A HUSTLER'S SON

A HUSTLER'S SON 2

THE FACE THAT LAUNCHED A THOUSAND BULLETS

YEAR OF THE CRACKMOM

THE UNUSUAL SUSPECTS

MISS WAYNE AND THE QUEENS OF DC

PAID IN BLOOD

RAUNCHY

RAUNCHY 2: MAD'S LOVE

RAUNCHY 3: JAYDEN'S PASSION

MAD MAXXX: CHILDREN OF THE CATACOMBS (EXTRA RAUNCHY)

JEALOUS HEARTED

QUITA'S DAYSCARE CENTER

QUITA'S DAYSCARE CENTER 2

DEAD HEADS

Drunk & Hot Girls

Pretty Kings

Pretty Kings 2: Scarlett's Fever

Pretty Kings 3: Denim's Blues

Hersband Material

Upscale Kittens

Wake & Bake Boys

Young & Dumb

Young & Dumb: Vyce's Getback

Tranny 911

Tranny 911: Dixie's Rise

First Comes Love, Then Comes Murder

Luxury Tax

The Lying King

Crazy Kind of Love

Silence of The Nine

Silence of The Nine II: Let There Be Blood

Prison Throne

Goon

Hoetic Justice

And They Call Me God

The Ungrateful Bastards

Lipstick Dom

A School of Dolls

Kali: Raunchy Relived The Miller Family

Skeezers

You Kissed Me Now I Own You

NEFARIOUS

The End. How To Write A Bestselling Novel in 30 Days

WWW.THECARTELPUBLICATIONS.COM

PUBLISHER'S NOTE:
This book is a work of fiction. Names, characters, businesses,
Organizations, places, events and incidents are the product of the
Author's imagination or are used fictionally. Any resemblance of
Actual persons, living or dead, events, or locales are entirely coincidental.

Library of Congress Control Number: 2016931720

ISBN 10: 0996209913

ISBN 13: 978-0996209915

Cover Design: Davida Baldwin www.oddballdsgn.com

www.thecartelpublications.com

First Edition

Printed in the United States of America

NEFARIOUS

BY

T. STYLES

What's Up Fam,

I can't believe we're already through with January 2016. We're preparing for Superbowl and Valentine's Day and before you know, it'll be Easter and Memorial Day. These months roll by extremely fast so stop every now and again to enjoy life. I'm serious! You don't want it to rush by and you haven't taken time out for yourself.

Aight…right into the book before you, "Nefarious". Man, this was a great crazy story! I haven't read about a person this mean since…*Raunchy* or *Silence of The Nine*. Wait until you get a load of Zoe! I'm sure you're gonna feel the same.

With that being said, and keeping in line with *Cartel Publicati*ons tradition, we want to give respect to a vet or a trailblazer paving the way. In this novel, we would like to recognize:

Cameron Newton

Cam Newton is the young quarterback for the *2016 NFC Champion North Carolina Panthers* football team. Now I know he plays for a team other than my faves—*Dallas Cowboys* and *Baltimore Ravens*—but I have MAJOR respect for this guy. He's a talented black quarterback in the *NFL* but in addition, he's a great humanitarian who loves helping and motivating children. Cam is a true example that no matter where you come from you can accomplish anything in life. Best of luck to Cam and his *Panthers* as they gear up for Superbowl 50.

Aight, get to it. I'll catch you in the next novel.

Be Easy!
Charisse "C. Wash" Washington
Vice President
The Cartel Publications
www.thecartelpublications.com
www.facebook.com/publishercwash
Instagram: publishercwash
www.twitter.com/cartelbooks
www.facebook.com/cartelpublications
Follow us on Instagram: Cartelpublications
#CartelPublications
#UrbanFiction
#PrayForCeCe
#CamNewton

CARTEL URBAN CINEMA'S 1st MOVIE

PITBULLS IN A SKIRT – THE MOVIE

NOW AVAILABLE:
DVD/AMAZON STREAMING

www.cartelurbancinema.com and
www.amazon.com
www.thecartelpublications.com

#Nefarious

NEFARIOUS – evil, immoral, criminal, wicked.

PROLOUGE

PRESENT

JUNE 24, 2015

The sun was beastly as it beamed heated rays through the windows of the black Cadillac ESV as it careened down the highway. Zoe Xavier's head rested in Tristan's lap, her glassy gaze toward the window.

Her fingers pushed against her neck while his hand covered hers to double up on pressure. After more blood oozed between their fingers he applied more force to disrupt the flow.

Seeing her on the brink of death tears fell from his eyes causing tiny trails within the splattered blood streams on his cheeks. "You can't die, ma. Not yet."

She tried to smile but she was suddenly introduced to more pain. "If I must die I'm okay, son. Really."

Tristan noticing how his mother's stare seemed to be more at peace than he wanted and was afraid she relented to death. "Hurry the fuck up, nigga!" He yelled at the driver who was doing his best to dodge traffic.

"I'm going as fast as I can, man," he said looking at Tristan's reflection in the rearview mirror.

Zoe, sensing Tristan's anxiety, placed her free hand on his, which still pushed at the gaping wound. She was extremely calm considering she lost so much blood that it coated the tan seats turning them dark burgundy.

"I'm okay, son," she whispered as she was finding it harder to speak. "I'm ready to die and I...I don't want you to worry about me."

"Ma, you can't go...we have so much to do.

I—"

"Tristan, the only thing I want." She took a deep breath because talking was strenuous and required energy she didn't possess. "The only thing I want is for you to look after your brother and love your girlfriend. So that she will take care of you and you can be happy."

Tristan took his eyes off of her and focused on the driver. His mother could talk recklessly all she desired but he wasn't about to accept her fate.

The veins on his temples pulsated and Tristan reached in his waist with his free hand, removed a .9 mili and shoved it against the back of the driver's head. "Let me make this clear." His body trembled. "If my mother dies in the back of this truck...you next."

Suddenly the large SUV gained new life as it zipped in and out of traffic.

Although Zoe realized the severity of her situation, she wasn't as anxious as Tristan to be saved. She took so many 'L's in life that she was looking forward to no more pain.

At the moment the right side of her face, permanently drifted downward due to a stroke years earlier, robbed her of her beauty. Only in her late 30s, she was the most hideous looking woman most had ever seen.

Zoe was ready to die.

Her life was complicated and long as she evolved to a monster.

As her body felt lighter her thoughts drifted on the past and how the evil that was Zoe Xavier came to be.

PART ONE

CHAPTER ONE

TEXAS

MARCH 2012

ZOE XAVIER – 31 YEARS OLD

"Chocolate & Cream"

They were waiting in line…

Standing against the basement wall like dogs waiting for meat while the first man tore at my 16-year-old daughter's womb. I stay tucked inside the closet watching because I wasn't sure if there was anything I could do to help.

Mrs. Xavier was present too, liquor pouring down the sides of her mouth as she cheered them on. She hated me so much that she was willing to go this far. When all I wanted to do was please her even though Mr. Xavier, her husband, cared for me.

Emma's light brown skin, mixed with their semen made her body shine grossly. She was naked on the floor, her legs spread as far apart as humanly allowed. The two long sandy braids she always wore were soaked in sweat and she trembled.

She didn't know I was there. Nobody did. But I wanted to go through the pain with her because I didn't deserve to hide. I should've done something. I should've said something but I was afraid.

Afraid Mrs. Xavier would send my kids away from the Xavier Estates because of the relationship I had with her husband. Out of all of the servants, which included twenty butlers, maids and handymen, I was the only one allowed to keep my children. Besides all three were Mr. Xavier's— another reason she hated me.

She never had one child although she tried.

While I, a slave, was given three.

I had my first baby at 12 years old, the next at 14 and then 16. The three of us shared one room in the home that was far more comfortable than where the other servants stayed, all bunked up in a room so hot and stuffy you could smell rancid odor stemming from everyone's body after a long day's work.

A maid once told us she heard out in the world people got paid for the work we did. But we never received compensation for anything and I was okay. I told her not to tell me any more of those stories because as long as my children were together and Mr. Xavier took care of us, I didn't need money.

Emma's eyes were open but her spirit looked like it left her to her own vices. Mr. Xavier didn't know about this because he was out of town on real estate business.

If only he knew.

I was hoping that the last one would be quick as the others. I was praying to God hard and then for some reason Emma rolled her head and looked toward the closet where I was hiding.

She'd seen me.

Could she hear my silent prayer?

The blank stare on her face went from emotionless to pain filled as she gazed my way. I saw the progression of her reaction as she went from agony to hate.

And I knew any love she had for me vanished.

My mind still on the rape I tried to think of something I could do to make Emma feel better. But she wouldn't talk to me.

On my hands and knees I was scrubbing the floor around the toilet in the master bathroom trying to think of a way to mend our relationship. Since Mrs. Xavier got her period, tiger blood stripes rolled down the sides of the bowl and I had to bleach them away.

She was nasty.

Even though I cleaned it everyday her room smelled of fish especially today since earlier one of the servants, a landscaper, had sex with her while she menstruated. If only Mr. Xavier knew the things she did while he was away.

She hated me but I would never tell.

Although sometimes I think she wanted me to.

When the bathroom was sparkling I grabbed a bottle of perfume that Mrs. Xavier used to spray on her vagina instead of washing after having sex. I was about to take it to the bedroom where the others were when the door opened and it crashed to the floor.

My heart dropped when I saw Mrs. Xavier standing before me. She had a bottle of beer in her hand and her eyes were red. She looked down at the broken perfume. I thought she was about to yell at me for it but she said, "I caught your youngest son sucking Carl's dick in the garage just now, Zoe." She grinned. "Did you know he was gay?"

My stomach flipped upon hearing the lies. "Ma'am...that's not true. I...he would..."

"I know what I saw." She frowned. "Seems like all of you are full of surprises. I even saw the glow in Emma's eyes as those men ravished her. And trust me, she loved it you know."

"Ma'am, please don't."

"Don't what, Zoe?" She yelled, spit flying from her lips. "She took all ten dicks like it was her life's work." She chuckled louder. "You should be proud."

I was silent and filled with anger.

"Come over here and give me a hug," Zoe. Her eyes were glassy.

I looked down at the scented glass on the floor. "But, ma'am..."

"I said come over here and give me a hug," she yelled. "And before you do, remove your shoes."

I sat on the toilet and removed my socks and tennis shoes. Slowly I walked over to her, glass digging into the soles of my feet.

All while she laughed.

CHAPTER TWO

ZOE

"Dreams Don't Do Anything But Kill"

I was washing the dishes when I gazed out of the window at the land encircling the mansion. The bottoms of my feet were cut and inflamed and I prayed Mr. Xavier returned today. Something told me if he didn't things would get worse for my family and me.

When I heard Celeste's voice coming behind me I moved quicker. Celeste, the most hateful servant of all stood next to me. Her beefy hands glued to her hips and her pinkish eyes that offset her inky black skin made her look like a monster. Along with the Xavier's she was the only one allowed to hit the servants and she did it often.

"I heard you made Mrs. Xavier upset today." She paused. "And you had to be punished."

It was a lie but I knew it was better to go along with it then make people angrier by saying the truth. "Yes, ma'am."

She smacked me and my mouth filled with salty liquid. When I looked down red blood drops mixed into the soapy water. I swallowed and wiped my lips with the back of my hand.

"You better hope she forgets about whatever you did later," She pointed in my face. "Karen here and she's been asking a lot of questions about your boys. With Clayton being 19 and Tristan 14, I'm surprised you've been able to keep them for that long."

"Yes, ma'am."

"Now get yo self together and go find your children. The Xavier's dinner party is starting in five minutes and I'm not about to let you fuck it up. Only for Mrs. Xavier's wrath to come down on all of us."

She stormed off.

When she left I released the water and looked at my face from the reflection in the window. My light skin was bruised around the mouth where she smacked me. Some of my hair eased from the long ponytail that I had hanging down my back.

I feel heavy because most everyone hates me and I don't know why. Mr. Xavier came into my room when I was 11. I didn't seek him out.

I learned to do what I must after my children were born to keep Mr. Xavier happy and he rewarded me by not shipping them away. But to make him happy meant Mrs. Xavier's sadness and there's no way around that.

I tried it all.

Massaged her feet. Cooked her favorite meals. Made homemade oils from the garden flowers and scented her pillows at night. But in the end she made it clear that she would never like me. And so every time Mr. Xavier was gone I was subjected constantly to a world of pain.

Mr. Xavier had more people than usual here for the party tonight. Including his best friend Mr. Porter Blackstone who brought his nephew Foster with him every time.

I didn't like Foster.

Foster did things with Emma that I chose not to know about. Since he taught her how to read, which none of us knew how to do but her, I let things slide. Besides, what power did I have over a daughter who was a servant just like me?

Foster was the only person who could put a smile on her face since she had been raped so I guess he served his purpose.

The appetizers had already been served and we were prepping for dinner when I noticed only Emma and my youngest son Tristan helping with prep.

Where was Clayton?

I don't know how he got to be so lazy but it was sad. Both of my boys were handsome and Clayton had deep young boy muscles and was strong. But out of nowhere he started getting shiftless. Something that could get him sent away.

It took some time but soon I realized that his attitude was as a result of his job responsibility changing recently. Since now he was in charge of washing the Xavier's cars in the inside port behind the mansion, this gave him access to television, which he wasn't allowed to watch normally.

None of us were.

One day he was one of the hardest workers and the next he started slacking off. Everyday he talked about an old TV show he told me he saw called 'The Wire'. In it he claimed black people sold drugs and because of it could live a similar lifestyle to the Xavier's.

"I think Mrs. Xavier is lying to us about black people, ma," He would say. *"I've seen TV shows where black people don't have to clean up behind whites. What if there is something else out there? Maybe we should run away and see."*

It always scared me when he said those words because if Mrs. Xavier ever heard him talking crazy she may finally convince Mr. Xavier to send them away, just to hurt me.

We had to be careful.

"So, Violet I see you have more help around here." Her name was Karen Bandicoot and she's Mrs. Xavier's best friend. That meant she automatically didn't like me. Today she doesn't frown at me like she usually does and I figure it's the Kettle One vodka Celeste kept refreshed in their glasses.

Celeste may be ugly and evil but I do believe she was the reason the Xavier's weren't so mean after their functions. Most times they were so drunk they never remember what happened the night before.

Arizona, another servant, was famous for using this privilege to her advantage. She was so pretty people said she may be my mama but no one was sure. Mrs. Xavier said what difference did it make who's your mother or father when I am God.

So we dropped it.

Anyway one day Arizona took advantage of the drunken days to say whatever was on her mind. One night after a function I heard her say, "Shut up, bitch," to Mrs. Xavier when she told her she was being sassy. And sure enough Mrs. Xavier didn't remember a thing the next morning.

"We actually have more servants than we need these days," Mrs. Xavier responded. "Maybe I can convince Edward to finally let the others go." She looked at me.

I felt stuck until Celeste walked past me and pinched the back of my arm.

"Well me and Steven thinking about getting servants ourselves. But with the new laws on trafficking it's hard to know who we can trust."

Mrs. Xavier leaned back in her seat and sucked her teeth. "Don't make anymore calls. Let me work on Edward. We have Clayton who's 19-years old and strong and his brother Tristan who's 14 who we can also let go."

A bundle of nerves, I dropped a plate of butter, angering Mrs. Xavier instantly.

She sighed. "What you doing now, dumb girl?" She shook her head. "I wish you could take her off of our hands but Edward would never part with her. She's his special one." She glared at me.

As the tension rose Celeste came out of nowhere and grabbed me by the ear. "Don't worry, Ma'am, I'll take care of her." She turned toward Emma. "Clean up that mess. Now."

Celeste hustled me toward the kitchen and through the large white swinging doors. She waited for the door's flow to stop before focusing on me. "I don't know what's on your mind but if you don't get it together you're gonna be shipped out of here," she whispered harshly before pinching my ear harder. "And considering all the problems you've caused over my lifetime it would be my pleasure."

From inside the kitchen I could still hear their voices while Celeste laid into me. I knew this would make her angrier, forcing her to rip my ear off, but I needed to get back out there and convince Mrs. Xavier that I was sorry for anything I did wrong.

I needed Mr. Xavier home now.

When I looked at Celeste for a moment I thought I saw pity as she looked at me. And then she cleared her throat and whispered, “Even if she gives them to Karen be grateful, Zoe. You’re the only one here who got to raise their kids. At the end of the day you are her property and you have to understand that.”

“But he promised he’d never take them from me,” I cried. “What if he listens to her this time?”

She grabbed me by my hand and yanked me to the wine cellar, closing the door behind us. Every shelf was filled with expensive wine and liquors and she pushed a wooden wine box toward me. It slid across the floor. “Sit down.”

I did.

“You don’t know what you’re doing by upsetting Mrs. Xavier so let me tell you a little history on this family.” She paused. “Mrs. Xavier’s family has been in this house for ages. Back in the day when the maiden name was Powell."

When we heard movement outside of the door we looked in the direction but heard nothing more.

"Like I was saying, Mrs. Xavier comes from a generation of slave owners. My family has been here since slavery was legal. But on January 1, 1863 my great-great-great grandmother had just gotten news that Negros were free."

My eyes widened because I didn't have a firm grasp on what *freedom* meant. All of my life I'd been here. Was there something else in the world?

"She was 30 years old and raised most of the Powell children. She never imagined freedom until the Emancipation Proclamation was signed. Her plan afterwards was to take her daughter, my great-great grandmother and go east where she heard niggers were treated better. Well John Powell, who she raised, snatched her out of the kitchen where the other slaves were discussing the news of their freedom."

She sighed and sat on a wooden crate although I knew I would have to help her get back up. She had to be at least 65 and her body was beat up.

"My great-great-great grandmother didn't know until that day but the Powell's had a wall of all the female slaves names written. Under the names were dashes, which represented the days they got their periods. The day they would be fertile."

I swallowed and was glued into the story.

"He raped her and when he was done he told her based on the new law he couldn't make her stay. But he also said if she could manage being a nigger woman with two children out in the world, which included the baby he was sure he made during that rape, then she was free to go. But if she stayed he'd take care of her for the rest of her life." She exhaled. "My great-great-great grandmother agreed to stay and when she walked back into the kitchen all of the other slaves were dead. The Powell family killed them and would've killed her too if she didn't agree. This family is so vicious they would rather the slaves be dead than free."

I put my hand over my mouth.

"Before long Edward Xavier married into the family and changed the estate name from Powell to Xavier." She paused. "But everything else is the same." She pointed at the floor. "These people still deal in humans."

"I'm confused."

"I don't see why. It's easy to understand." She sighed. "My great-great-great grandmother stayed and although John Powell wife was in the same home he made many children with my ancestor. And it's because this is our life, it's all we know." She paused. "I've never been out of this house and I don't know what's going on in the world. Except the conversations I overheard with Edward and his friends shows us of black people being killed by police on the streets and that's enough for me. But I've long since given up on my dreams about having a life anywhere beyond the Xavier Estates." She pointed at me. "You better get rid of your dreams too. For yourself and your children."

"But I don't understand what this has to do with my kids."

"Because you have sex with Mr. Xavier, you believe that gives you the right to speak up to white folks and that's a mistake. These people are dangerous; Zoe and they will kill you. They killed my father for having similar dreams when he lived here." She paused. "Dreams don't do anything but kill the soul and in this house the soul is all you have to survive."

I felt weaker because I knew she was right.

"Black folk ain't nothing but a floorboard for white folk to stand on. Get used to that and you'll find peace. Think of yourself as anything other than that and you're in for a world of pain."

Mr. Xavier came home.

Exhausted.

And I felt immediate relief.

In time for the dinner party, the entire time I prepared his plate Mrs. Xavier stared at me across the room, reminding me with her eyes not to say a word about the rape. But now I had more troubles to worry about, like my children being given away and only he could help.

After the party I got Mr. Xavier ready for the night. He was bathed and clothed in pajamas sprayed with lavender oil. Earlier in the evening, Mrs. Xavier jumped in bed without washing and had liquor and vomit stuck on her clothing. I didn't like it but I had to clean her up too. When they both were tucked in, I got on my knees, on his side of the bed, ready to throw myself at his mercy.

His cheeks were red and I could tell he was going to be in pain tomorrow with a hangover. "After all of these years, you're still beautiful." He said touching my face with his warm palm.

I could hear Mrs. Xavier snoring, which meant we were free to talk. "Thank you. You know it's my life's work to please you."

He smiled. "Something is on your mind. What is it, Zoe?"

I swallowed the fear, knowing Mr. Xavier had always been on my side. "It's about my kids."

He removed his hand and placed it on his belly. "What about them?"

I saw Mrs. Xavier stir and we both remained still. When I heard her snoring again I spoke freely. "I think she is going to give them to Karen."

"Give them to Karen?" He laughed. "Says who?"

"She said she's going to give them away just to hurt me and I'm afraid."

He laughed. "I'm not sure what went on while I was gone but she does not have the authority to give anybody anything." He touched my face again. "No matter what, those children have my blood and I will not see my bloodline shipped away from this home. I told you that."

I smiled and wanted to say more. "There's something else."

"What is it?"

I swallowed the lump in my throat. "Mrs. Xavier, she, well sir..."

"Zoe, just say it."

"She let her cousins rape, Emma."

He popped up in bed and looked down at me. "Zoe, you better be certain before making such claims to me. This could ruin our relationship forever."

I looked up at him. "Sir, have you ever known me to lie?"

CHAPTER THREE

EMMA XAVIER – 16 YEARS OLD

"This Time I'm Willing"

His touch is like a cooled coat of wax on my skin. His fingers pale but strong; moved up my legs like ice along a glass table. I love him; want to be with him more than anything. The feeling is stronger because I know he wants me back.

Lying on top of me he looked down into my eyes, we were on the floor in the basement, a yellow towel underneath us and we'd just finished making love. It was the same floor where men ravaged my body against my will, but this time I'm willing.

"You were wetter than normal, Emma," Foster said, kissing me on the lips. "Why?"

I looked up at him before running my fingers through his soft blonde hair. I get lost into the piercing blues of his eyes every time. "You do it to me." I ran my fingers down his back. "Can I do anything to please you again? If so just say the word."

He smiled. "What did I do to deserve you?"

I squinted. "You're playing right?"

"I don't play with you, Emma. You know that." He kissed my chin and grabbed one of my plaits. I kept my golden brown hair in two long braids that ran down my back. "You know that I'm serious."

I exhaled, although not fully because his body was on top of me. "You deserve me because you've done so much. You taught me how to read when my mother wouldn't even allow me to hold a book because she's too afraid of what Mrs. Xavier might say." I sighed. "Her weaknesses makes me sick and I'd give anything not to be like her."

"Why do you hate her so much?"

I closed my eyes and tried to squeeze the memory of seeing her watch all of those men climb on me and do nothing. Foster didn't know because I never told. She didn't do anything and for that I hate her immensely. "Because she doesn't deserve my love. I won't say anything more."

He nodded. "I know it runs deeper...with your mother and all...but Mrs. Xavier is dangerous, Emma. More dangerous than her husband if you can believe that. Zoe didn't want you to get caught with that book and—"

"She's afraid, Foster! My mother's afraid to better herself. She's afraid to eat an extra piece of meat if the Xavier's don't give it to her. She's afraid of life. And I'm ashamed to call her my mother."

"You may be judging her too harshly." He paused. "Everyday I come home from college I talk to you about the world. I tell you how things are out there so that you can see it through my eyes. But your mother is right. In the world black people can't walk down the street without being killed. Black people can't have jobs or children. You're better off here where the Xavier's can take care of you."

"Maybe I would believe I was better off if you lived here too." I paused. "If I have to be a servant I'd rather belong to you. Not the Xavier's. They have no respect for me."

He laughed. "We've been friends all of our lives, Emma but your mother just wants you to be safe. And you're safe here."

"Just friends?"

He smiled. "You know how I feel about you. Just like you're risking it all to be with me I'm risking it all by sleeping with you. My mother isn't racist but she would never accept me being with a black woman."

"Then how can she not be racist?"

He rose and grabbed his pants that were lying on the floor across the room. Scared he might walk out forever I jumped up, wrapped the towel around me and hugged him tightly from behind. I kissed his pale warm back and squeezed him again. "I love you for eternity, Foster."

"It's okay, Emma." He turned around and faced me. "You're entitled to your feelings." He grabbed my chin and kissed me. "There's no need to be afraid, I'm not going anywhere."

"Then why does it seem like you're mad?"

"Because I'm entitled to my feelings too." He paused. "My mother isn't racist. She's a realist and there's a difference."

I let him go. "You're right and I apologize." I paused. "Foster, did you mean it when you said I could run away and be with you next year? If I found a way out of here."

He placed his cool hands on my face, sucked my bottom lip and looked into my eyes. "If you make it out I'll be waiting."

"Sis, you have to come with me now. Ma says it's important." When I saw Tristan's hysterical look after he ran downstairs I knew something was wrong.

I quickly looked for my clothing. "What's going on?" I hopped around as I slid my maid's uniform over my head.

"I don't know but it looks serious." Tristan gazed at Foster before looking away. He scratched his golden curly fro and tucked his hands in his back pocket. My brother had the prettiest hair, unlike mine, which is stringy, forcing me to keep it in two braids all the time. "Hello, sir."

"You don't have to speak to me formally, Tristan. I told you that before. I'm just a friend." Foster walked over to me, snaked his arm around my back and kissed me on the lips. "I'm leaving out the back door. I left a new book for you in your mattress, under the bed. I'll see you in a few days." He shook Tristan's hand and walked out the door while I buttoned my dress.

Feeling my brother's prying eyes I said, "Don't look at me like that, Tristan."

"I don't have an opinion. I just don't want you to get hurt."

"I won't get hurt, trust me. He cares about me." When I was dressed Tristan took me by the hand and led me up the stairs. "This seems weird, with mother, Tristan. She didn't give a clue?"

"Nope but it doesn't look good," he said.

We were deep in the wine cellar, behind the largest shelf, where mother and my oldest brother Clayton, who I hated, stood. Unlike Tristan he did everything in his power to make life miserable for me. He'd do stuff like lie about me not doing a chore or threaten to tell the Xavier's about Foster and me having sex. He was as mean as a snake.

"So you topped your white boyfriend off and now you can finally grace us with your presence?" Clayton said sarcastically. He rubbed his baldhead before smoothing his goatee with his fingers.

I was about to rush up on him when Tristan held me back. "Don't do it, sis."

"Yeah, listen to our faggedy brother. He knows the right way to be around me. Because you can walk over here if you want to and you'll get that face slapped."

My eyes widened. I didn't know anybody knew about Tristan but me and Tristan held my hand.

Surprisingly my mother remained silent although I know she heard him.

"Children," mother whispered. "This is serious."

When I looked into her eyes I could tell she'd been crying. I stepped to her. "What's going on?"

She grabbed my hand and I snatched away.

I hated her touching me.

She cleared her throat and said, "Mrs. Xavier is talking about separating us and I think she plans to do it over the next few days."

My eyes widened. "Separating us." I repeated. "But, I thought you said he would never do that because you were his favorite. And that we don't have anything to worry about."

"Dad wouldn't do that," Tristan said. "He cares about us too much."

I don't know why Tristan called him dad. He may have done things for us and treated us better than the others but we were still servants. If I was truly respected as a daughter they would've never raped me.

"Like I said it's not him it's her. That's why I called you all here."

"What is it, mother?" Tristan asked. "Because we're all willing to do whatever we have to, to stay."

She frowned. "Are you really?" She paused. "Because there's a rumor going around that you like boys, Tristan. Is that true?"

Wow.

She did know.

Tristan remained quiet and he seemed ashamed. I knew my brother liked men but I loved him anyway.

"Mother, people around here make up stories all the time. They are just angry at what Mr. Xavier does for you. I think this is the real reason she wants to get rid of us. It's your entire fault. "

Clayton laughed. "So you're still mad at ma about them white boys climbing on top of you and yet you fucking Foster on the same floor." He chuckled louder. "You need to get over it, sis. All they took was some pussy."

I felt every vein in my body pulsate with rage. Ever since Clayton had been watching TV he talked and acted differently, using some words I didn't understand. "I hate you."

"Fuck you too." He responded back.

"Children, let's not fight each other. We have to be smart about our next move." She paused. "Now Mr. Xavier is going to talk to her when he comes back. He doesn't want to upset her too much until then."

"He's leaving again?" I frowned. "He just got back tonight."

"I know. He'll be gone again for a few weeks and then he'll be here for good. Then he'll talk to her about separating us and what happened to you, Emma. But we need to stay out of her way and make sure everything is in top shape."

I crossed my arms over my body. "I don't want him to talk about what happened to me. I want to do the move we discussed, mother. I want to leave."

"Emma—"

"No mother!" I yelled. "Let's talk about the fact that you can't protect us while he's not here. If we don't do something now I fear we won't have a choice." I paused. "Besides, all of Clayton's house work is going to fall on me and Tristan since he hasn't lifted a finger in months."

Clayton grinned.

"Please stop it, children. This plan includes us getting little sleep. But we will let Mrs. Xavier see that having us here, together, is invaluable."

"Why don't we just leave?" I continued to beg. "Why not take a chance on whatever is out there?"

"Run where, Emma? I've never been outside of the fields of the Estates and neither have you. Where will we go? Where will we live?"

I lowered my brows. "But don't you even want to try? Don't you even want to see if something is out there better?" I pointed at the window. "I'm tired of living here, mother. What if there's an entire world waiting and you're wasting it here?" I yelled.

Mother walked up to me and grabbed both of my hands. She stared so deeply at me I had to look away. I know she didn't want us to be a part but there was no way I could put myself through another rape.

"Emma, we can't run. This is home and Mr. Xavier would be heartbroken." She paused. "We have to stay and fight."

"I'd rather try to escape and die while living then stay and die a slow death. It's time to leave, ma. You and me both know it."

"As much as I hate to hear Emma she's right," Clayton said. "I'm trying to tell you that Mrs. Xavier is playing us, ma. Got us thinking that the world hates us. Well I see TV shows and I know there's something out there for us too. Like she said, why not take our chances and get out of this place?"

I hated the new way he talked but I'm glad he agreed with me.

When I looked into my mother's eyes I could tell she was going to die here. This was the first time any of us had spoken about running away and she couldn't handle it.

"Either you leave with me or I'm leaving without you," I said.

CHAPTER FOUR

ZOE

"This Time You'll Experience Sincere Pain"

Mr. Xavier was gone but Mrs. Xavier seemed calmer today and I was relieved. Her facial expression was fixed like she just received good news.

I think I had an idea what made her so happy. My kids and me rose early yesterday and moved all the unwanted trash from the shed and I called Mr. Highland, the only number on speed dial I was allowed to press, to come haul it away. Then we wiped the shed down and disinfected it so that Mrs. Xavier could do her ceramic sculptures that she use to love.

As I rubbed Mrs. Xavier's feet I looked up at her every so often to see if she was still smiling and she was. "How are you, ma'am? You look happy."

She smiled. "Actually, Zoe I couldn't be better." She wiggled her toes.

I wanted to know if there were any plans to move my children away but I also didn't want to press the issue. She was normally so uptight that I could take things too far and in an instant she would turn vicious. "Mrs. Xavier, did you see what me and the kids did to the shed? We cleaned it up and made it really nice."

"Yes, Zoe," she smiled. She leaned her head backwards and closed her eyes. "I saw. Thank you very much." She paused. "But I been meaning to ask you something."

"Anything," I said excitedly.

"Has Clayton had a woman yet?" She grinned. "Because lately I've been juicing up just thinking about those muscular arms and that baldhead." She moaned and licked her lips. "I always wondered how it would be to fuck my husband's son. I bet he feels better." She glared at me.

The last thing I wanted was her around my son and I felt sick. "Please, ma'am, he's still so young."

"And so were you, when you seduced Edward." She snapped.

"But I was 11 ma'am."

"Do you love my husband?" She opened her eyes and stared down at me. "Because you seem very in tune with his needs, sometimes at the expense of mine."

This was turning badly. I massaged her big toe and considered the question fully before answering. I didn't want to walk into a trap to make things worse for my children. "I love both of you, ma'am. You allowed me to stay with my children and that means a lot. Especially since everyone isn't given the same privilege."

She laughed. "Answer the question, Zoe." She was firm and sounded irritated.

"No, ma'am. I don't love him in that way. I care for him like I care for you but that's it."

She laughed. "Then why is it every time I turn around you're in our bedroom? Or fucking him in that cellar?" She pushed the sole of her foot in my face and stood up. I smelled the corn chip scent of her toes. Before I knew it her fist came down on my eye. I could feel the blood rushing to the surface as she followed up with a kick to my gut. "You don't know your place, Zoe. You never have and I feel the need to clear things up for you. You work for me...you are not my equal."

She's beaten me before but never after sounding so nice. I felt like I walked into a trap. After leading me on to believe that today was one of the good days, she continued to pound until she was so tired her sweat dripped on my back as I curled up in a ball.

"Mrs. Xavier, please stop..." I cried.

"I know you don't understand why I have to beat you. You aren't smart enough to comprehend so I'm not surprised. But if I don't punish you, you'll think it's okay for you to rebel against someone who is taking care of you. I rule your life, Zoe. Me. The moment you start understanding this I'll show you mercy but not until then."

"You're right, Mrs. Xavier. You're right."

"I know what you're doing now." Her breaths were heavy and although I couldn't see her due to hiding my face, I could feel her rage. "You think you can seduce me like you do Edward? Well it won't work. This time you'll experience sincere pain, every second, every minute of your life when your children are finally shipped away you will be miserable. It will be my life's work."

I felt like I'd been smacked in the head with a dumbbell. "Mrs. please...please don't separate us. You can beat me if you must. I don't care but not my kids."

She laughed hysterically, I guess building enough energy to mock me further. "Tomorrow when you wake up you will find that each of your children, not just the two you thought, will be gone. And there is nothing Edward can do to help you."

CHAPTER FIVE

EMMA

"The Elephant And The Rope"

I stood over my mother with tears running down my cheeks as she sat on a wooden wine case in the cellar. Don't know why I'm crying. Not sure if I even care that she was beaten. Because she's light skin like us her bruises were red with a hint of blue.

I don't know what happened between her and Mrs. Xavier but I know nobody's going to sell me. "Mother, what now?" I mopped the tears away roughly. "If we stay we're never going to see each other again. Is that what you want?"

"Emma, it's not that easy." She paused. "If we leave without telling Mr. Xavier he would be devastated. He'll worry about us."

I breathed heavily and could feel my nostrils widening and closing. "Well are you gonna stay here? Because I'm not moving with another family. I won't."

She sat up and looked up at me. "Emma, please just listen." She grabbed my hands and I noticed her palms were clammy. She was so scared she was sweating. "I'm begging you to let me talk to Mr. Xavier first. I know it sounds crazy but he's always looked out for us in the past."

I stormed away and leaned against the wall. "You let them rape me. You let them rape me while you watched. And you really think I'm going to stick around for more?"

"Don't do anything crazy, Emma." She sniffled. "I'm begging."

"If by crazy you mean stay here and let someone sell me off then so be it. I just wanted you to know that I'm gone tonight. I don't expect you to care too much since you love him more than you ever loved me."

When she stood up I got a closer view of her face and it made me sick. The only thing any of us knew was the Xavier Estates. But being with Foster has shown me that I can do anything and I'm going for it no matter what. "But what will you do out there, Emma?"

"I have Foster's address and I'm going to stay with him in his guest house until I can figure things out." I exhaled.

"He gave you his address?"

"Yes," I cleared my throat. "Yes...um...he wanted me to have it."

"Well what about your brothers?"

"Clayton's leaving with me but he isn't staying for long. Tristan's going too. I guess they'd rather be out there then to stay in this house another day. And you should feel the same." I stomped up the stairs.

The hallway leading toward the backyard was dark and dank. I saw spider webs accumulating in the corners because nobody ever came down here. Not even us to clean it. This place made my skin crawl and I could feel the spirit of the slaves who died here. In a way they were making me stronger.

Clayton was already next to me but I was afraid mother got to Tristan and he would not come. If I left him I would never be able to live with myself because I knew I had to go with or without him. "He scared," Clayton chuckled under his breath. "The faggy gonna stay with ma and be her bitch. I'm not even surprised." He was wearing a white t-shirt that his muscles seemed to bulge out of and his baldhead had been recently shaved.

I never understood how he was so muscular since he didn't do anything.

I rolled my eyes and sighed. "You don't know what you're talking about. And you should be happy I'm even allowing you to go with me. Especially after the living hell you've put me through."

"You know I was just fucking with you."

"How would I know when you never told me?" I paused. "You're very mean to me and Tristan. I probably won't see you again after we separate but in case you remain with Tristan you better ease up on him. He's not going to be your punching bag forever."

"Yeah aight. What I want to know is how come we sitting in this hallway waiting on him?" He paused. "You know he not coming. We might as well leave."

"What you gonna do when we get to his house? Because you won't be staying with me."

"I'm gonna find a connect, get some drugs and be a boss."

I looked at him and laughed. "Clayton, stop believing everything you see on TV. Foster told me everything you see is not real."

"Like you know."

"I know more stuff about the world than you."

"We gonna see who's going to make it and who doesn't." He paused. "I'm gonna be good. Trust me."

About five minutes later we were about to leave when Tristan came into view, holding one suitcase and my mother's hand. His wild curly hair partially covering his eyes. I placed my fingers over my heart and ran up to him. "You weren't going to leave me were you?" He asked.

"Never," I said hugging him tightly. When we separated I looked at my mother.

"Ma's coming with us." He said cheerfully. "Isn't that good?" He removed a black rubber band from his wrist and tamed his hair into a man bun that sat on top of his head.

My eyes widened because I knew the last thing my mother wanted was to leave Mr. Xavier. I appreciated that he did things for us but what if there was more? She never told me but I knew she loved him even though he would never love her back. "I thought you were gonna stay," I said to her.

She looked at Tristan. "I'm going wherever my kids are."

"Then we better hurry." When I touched my pocket I realized the key to open the back door wasn't with me. How could I be so foolish? "What the fuck?" I whispered.

"What?" Clayton asked stepping up behind me.

"The key to get out...I left it upstairs."

Clayton placed his hands on the sides of his face.

"I knew this was a bad idea," my mother said. "Let's just go back."

I felt like a ton of wet cement had been poured over my head. I would never see my family again and it was my entire fault. My mother said we would be leaving tomorrow so this was my only chance and I ruined it. The house is too busy to escape in the daytime.

The three of us were heading back but Tristan remained at the door. "Did you try to open it, Emma?" he said with his back faced us, while focusing on the knob.

I walked up to him. "You know the door isn't open. They always talk about how all the doors in the house are locked."

"But did you try?"

I hadn't because I knew there was no need. Just to prove him wrong I twisted the knob and it turned. I felt like my breath was taken away. I placed my hand over my mouth. "Oh my God, it was open all this time." I hugged him and could not contain myself. Mr. and Mrs. Xavier probably knew we were so trained to be afraid that we would never leave and until now they were right.

Thanks to Tristan it was a big mistake.

I opened the door and we all bolted out into the darkness. I ran as fast as I could with the only noise being the sounds of their breath rushing behind me. Branches crackled under our feet and the songs of crickets chirping made me feel uneasy. Sweat drops formed on my forehead and rolled down my face and into my eyes.

Suddenly I was starting to believe that maybe this was a mistake. When I saw what I thought was a road ahead my heart rate increased. It seemed like we were running forever until I heard someone's voice.

"Zoe Xavier!" When I looked around I saw Celeste and knew my world was over. Her hands were crawled into fists and she seemed angrier than ever. She walked up to my mother and said, "Where do you all think you're going?"

Although it was dark the moonlight still shone over her pinkish eyes and out here she looked more evil. Celeste was the vilest out of all of the servants and I didn't trust her. She was always bossing me or my mother around and it was clear she hated us. No matter how angry she was I was not going back without a fight. I wanted to be with Foster and nothing would stop me.

"We're...we're leaving, Celeste," my mother said. "Mr. Xavier knows all about it. I was just..."

She laughed and her voice mixed in with animal noises in the distance that sounded off the night. "You think I'm stupid to believe that Edward is letting his property leave without telling me? You think I don't know the children supposed to be shipped off tomorrow?"

"Come on, mother," I said. "We have to go."

"You're not going anywhere, girl." She pointed at her. "Before I give you the okay."

"Celeste, please let us go," my mother pleaded moving closer to her. "All we want is to stay to—"

Celeste raised her hand, silencing my mother. "There ain't a lot of time so I'm gonna make what I got to say quick." Her evil expression softened a little. "I'm...I'm proud of you." Her gaze fell upon me. "Of all of you for being able to do something I never could." She sighed. "This is the farthest I've ever gotten from the Estates and I didn't know this much beauty existed." She looked out into the distance. "But now I do."

"I don't understand," my mother said.

"I can't explain a lot right now but take this." Celeste reached into her pocket and handed my mother a white envelope. My mother opened it and inside was some cash held together by a piece of notebook paper with writing. "When you get somewhere safe have somebody read it for you." She looked at me. "Like Emma."

"Why are you helping us?" I asked.

She exhaled. "I've been here all of my life. And I used fear to keep those who didn't have the strength to leave because I didn't want them hurt. I didn't want them killed. But you all are different. And that deserves a little help. If you stay together you can go all the way. But be smart and don't let anybody know about your past as slaves, they'll use it against you." She exhaled. "I can't explain a lot to you now but you need to know that I'm your mother, Zoe."

I looked over Celeste's head thinking someone was coming to pull us back but still I saw no one. I knew we had to hurry regardless because time was not on our side.

My mother covered her mouth after hearing the news. I guess she was as shocked as I was considering everyone thought Arizona was her mama. "You're my mother?"

Celeste looked behind her. She sighed. "You have to leave now. Everything you want to know about me is in that letter." She shoved my mother and then me toward the road. "Now all of you...go. Get out of here. While you still can."

Using the money Celeste gave us we caught a ride with a man inside a truck big enough to fit all of us. It felt so weird to be in a vehicle. And I had to keep my head down to avoid throwing up. My mother said her temples throbbed. Tristan vomited and Clayton complained of dizziness. I was glad the ride was over but knew with time we would all get use to it.

My mother was jittery and nervous when we made it to Foster's. Tristan was doing all he could to calm her down but it was Clayton who convinced her that everything would be okay. Now that I was at his place I agreed to let them stay for one night because Foster and my plans never consisted of them being in the picture.

Tristan was the only person I wanted to remain in contact with but I was good if I never saw my mother or Clayton again. When we made it to the back of Foster's house, I knocked on the door softly like we talked about many times. Although this was the first time I ever ran away, Foster and me developed a plan a while ago. If I ever escaped from the Xavier's house I was to call.

He didn't know I looked at the address on his driver's license one day and knew where he lived. I wanted to surprise him instead of calling and I knew he would be happy to see me.

I knocked on the door closest to the garage in the back of the house and turned toward my family. "Now I need everyone to be quiet when we get inside. He doesn't know all of you were coming."

"Does he even know you coming?" Clayton said.

"It doesn't matter. He's going to be happy to see me." I rolled my eyes. "I can't say the same for you."

I focused on the door. Clayton had his muscular arm around my mother and Tristan nodded. When Foster didn't come right away I knocked three more times, until I could hear Foster talking on the phone inside. He sounded upbeat and just hearing his voice put me in a better mood.

After a minute he pulled the door open and the smile he held before seeing me vanished. “Emma.” He looked over my head at my family and back at me. “What are you doing here?” His nostrils flared. His pale skin reddened.

He was being shy so I rushed up to him. “I finally did it.” I released him and hugged him again. “We can finally be together.”

“Aren’t you just thrilled?” Clayton said sarcastically.

“Shut up!” I yelled pointing at him.

I focused on Foster again. He smiled although not fully. I was starting to think he wasn’t happy to see me. Until I thought about my family. Our plans never included them so he was probably upset about their presence. I wasn’t worried because I would explain my plan to get rid of them soon.

“Clayton, aren’t you happy?” I grabbed one of his hands.

“Uh...yes...of course.” He opened the door. “Come inside.”

We piled into the house and I was surprised that this was the guesthouse he talked about so much. It wasn't as big as the living room at the Estates but it was larger than the room we shared.

When we stepped deeper into the house I hugged him again. I couldn't keep my hands off of him. "This is beautiful." I looked around and my family stood behind me.

"Uh...thank you." He placed the phone against his ear. "Let me call you back, Amanda." He dropped the cell phone in his pocket.

Who was Amanda?

"So...how did you leave?" He asked.

I grabbed his hand and looked into his eyes. "It was easier than I thought, Foster. The back door was unlocked. Had I known I could've left at anytime we would've been together much sooner. It's like we talked about one day...you know...the elephant and the rope."

"What's the elephant in the rope?" Clayton asked with a frown.

Foster cleared his throat and stuffed his hands inside his pockets. I wished Clayton did a better job of being silent but he didn't. "In

Southeast Asia baby elephants are tamed by being tied to a tree with a rope. In the beginning the elephant tries to get free but after awhile he believes he can't and stops trying. Even when untied."

Clayton frowned and scratched his baldhead. "So what does that got to do with this?"

My family is so dumb. Unlike them I didn't spend the little free time we had in the Xavier Mansion playing drinking games or having sex. I learned everything I could from Foster. I had dreams of being his wife like the women in my books and nothing was going to stop me.

"It just means that the elephant was bound when he was young but when he was an adult the rope wasn't his biggest enemy. His mind was."

"So why didn't he go?" Clayton asked.

"Because he was tamed." He rubbed his temples. "Emma, we must talk in private. Now."

CHAPTER SIX

ZOE

"Did My Daughter Make A Mistake Trusting You"

He doesn't want us here.

I don't blame him. His uncle, Porter Blackstone, would never allow him to keep us here. He was a trust fund baby, something I learned by eavesdropping at the mansion one day. With us here his money was in jeopardy I was certain.

When I sat down I watched Clayton grab the remote and turn on the TV I felt sick to my stomach. He fell too easily into this mode of not working and I was worried for his future if we were going to remain free. What if they brought us back to the Xavier Estates? I didn't think about what it meant to run clearly and I fell in over my head. It felt like someone was pushing water into my brain and it was about to burst.

"Mother, can I do anything for you?" Tristan asked sitting next to me. "I can ask Foster for some ice water."

"Just leave me alone right now, Tristan." I stroked my throbbing temples. "I have to process everything."

"But do you want me to see if he can give you some water?" He moved closer. "Or some pain medicine."

"Didn't she say just leave her alone?" Clayton yelled. "That's your problem now, you carry yourself like a female. Back the fuck up. You so close to her you getting on my nerves."

"Clayton, please don't fight," I said raising my head. It felt like the room was spinning. "Just...just...stop it."

Clayton glared at me. "No, ma he needs to hear the truth because he doesn't have the protection of the Xavier's no more." He frowned at Tristan. "You gotta toughen up if you want to live in this world." He pointed at him. "I haven't been out long but I've heard stories and they'll eat a nigga like you alive."

Emma twisted the end of one of her French braids as she walked out from the back. Foster hung behind her. "He says you can stay for two nights but after that you have to go." She crossed her arms over her chest and looked down at the floor. "I'm sorry."

"But where we gonna live?" Tristan asked. "We don't know anybody."

I looked at my daughter and could tell she was done with us. She got her wish and that was to be with Foster. Whatever happened to us was our own problem. "I guess we have to figure it out," I said.

I was asleep on the sofa but I heard Foster's voice in the kitchen. Even at Xavier Estates he was never one for whispering. He was always the loudest person in the room and his arrogance sickened me. Why Emma gravitated toward him I will never understand.

"I don't know where they are," Foster said into the phone. "But they've never been out on their own...maybe they'll come back. Is uncle Xavier okay?"

There was an extended pause and I knew the conversation was about us. I couldn't sleep all last night, wondering what would happen. I guess I'm about to find out.

"Uncle Porter I'm not lying," He continued. "I don't know where they are."

Pause.

"Yes, I was friendly with Emma but we didn't have the kind of relationship you think. The only thing I—"

Pause.

"I would never go against the family for anyone, uncle. Especially not for niggers."

Pause.

"Yes, uncle, if I find out something I'll let you know." He paused. "Yes, sir." I heard him place the cell phone down and I pretended to be just waking. From the sofa I looked behind me and he was leaning against the refrigerator. His upper body was slumped forward and I could tell he was battling with himself.

I didn't trust my family being here, not even Emma so I had to learn more. "Good morning,

Foster." I stood by the doorway. "Is everything okay? You look troubled."

He stood straight, his body rigid. "You know how to make eggs right?"

"I've been making them most of my life."

He opened the refrigerator, pulled out eggs and cheese and sat them on the counter. "Make them."

I walked deeper into the kitchen. "How do you like 'em?"

"Scrambled. Heavy on the cheese."

I opened a few cabinets until I found a red bowl. I cracked three eggs and things felt awkward as he stood behind me, watching. I figured he wanted to talk more then I did. "Is everything okay, Foster?" I beat the yolk softly. "You're not yourself this morning."

He looked at me. "What's the plan? For Emma and the others."

I shrugged. "Playing it by ear I guess."

"You're going to need to do more than just that."

"True, but it's a start."

He sighed. "Are you able to take care of yourself alone, Zoe? You've spent your life working for someone else. Having someone take care of you. Do you know how hard things are out there?" he pointed at the window. "How do you know you're not making a mistake by escaping?"

"Do *you* know how to care for yourself?" I walked to the refrigerator and grabbed the butter.

He frowned. "What do you mean?"

"Not trying to be disrespectful, just saying that you're very young to be advising me on life. I'm guessing you can't know much more than I do right about now."

I turned the stove on. "But I've been out there," he said. "I've dealt with other people and I'm telling you it's hard. Maybe you should—"

"Are you gonna tell your uncle we're here?" I decided not to play games anymore. "Are you going to hand over Emma?"

"I care about your daughter and would never—"

"Are you going to tell your uncle that we're here or not?" I asked firmly. I'm not sure where the boldness stemmed from. Maybe Mrs. Xavier was right. Maybe I didn't know my place. "Did my daughter make a mistake trusting you?"

Suddenly I spotted a steak knife in the sink next to where I stood by the stove. Slowly I slid my hand into the base and clutched the black handle without pulling it out. I've never killed a living thing in my life. I was too afraid and now isn't much different. But if I even thought he would contact his uncle and rip my family apart I had all intentions on using it.

"You're safe here." He walked toward the exit of the kitchen, stopped and cleared his throat. "I mean...you're safe for now."

I released the knife.

He had no idea how close he came to dying.

Truthfully, neither did I.

The door was cracked open and I saw Emma tossing around inside Foster's room. I let myself inside and sat on the edge of the bed. "Emma...we need to talk."

She popped up, rubbed her eyes and used the sheet to cover her body. "What are you doing in here, mother?"

"I think we should leave today. I don't feel safe." She rolled her eyes and I was immediately reminded at how much she hated me. "Emma, I think Foster told his uncle. If he finds us we'll have to go back. You too."

She eased out of bed naked. Stomping over to the dresser she grabbed a big t-shirt from a closet and slipped it over her cream colored frame. I noticed it didn't hide all of her plump rear. "First off Foster would never do something like that because he loves me." She re-braided one of her plaits that unraveled. "Second, why would you care if we were caught? You obviously want to be back in that God-awful place anyway. So you can be up under your master again." She smirked.

Where had she learned to talk so cold?

"I woke up early, Emma and he didn't know I was listening while he was on the phone. He was talking to his uncle. If they get us we will be separated. Is that what you want? Isn't the purpose for running to stay free?"

She laughed at me. “I don’t know why I’m humoring this, mother but for you I will. Let me go talk to Foster and—”

“No!” I yelled before simmering down. I wasn’t use to screaming but lately I found myself not being able to contain my temper, especially when it came to her. I had to remember that she was damaged and it was partially my fault. “Emma, we can’t let him know that we’re aware. I’m telling you he’s a snake.”

She sighed and fanned her hand. “I’m going to go talk to my man, mother. I need this cleared up before you pop a blood vessel and ruin what I’m building here. Just give me a few minutes and I’ll be back.”

CHAPTER SEVEN

EMMA

"For The Rest Of My Life"

My mother is laughable.

She really wants me to be the frightened shell of a woman she's become but I refuse. First I needed to clear up this foolishness with Foster.

When I walked out into the garden Foster was sitting in front of the rose bush in a metal chair. I looked around and was stunned at the colors. There were amazing specks of red petals, pink, white and more. He spoke about this garden many times but seeing it now was surreal.

Was I really free?

And would I stay that way.

When I walked up from behind him I placed my hands on his shoulders and massaged lightly. Whenever he was at the Xavier Estate, to justify us spending so much time together I would pretend to be giving him massages. And since I gave them to everyone at the Estates and was good at it, no one batted an eye when we snuck off to make love.

He allowed me to stroke him for several minutes in silence before exhaling and gently pulling my hand so that I could sit on his lap. “Thank you…that was nice.” He kissed me.

“I love you, Foster.” I squinted to shield the sun from shining into my eyes. “And I will for the rest of my life.”

“I know.”

“And I’ll do anything for you, go anywhere with you too. All you have to do is ask.” He nodded and then his gaze fell off of me and onto the flowers. I immediately felt a sense of loss but I couldn’t understand why. “Is something wrong?”

“What could be wrong if you’re here with me?”

I smiled, although not as brightly as I had in the past when he said such sweet things. “Then why do you look troubled?”

He sighed. “There are a lot of things that go on out here, in the world. Things you have been shielded from. I tried to teach you, Emma. I wanted you to learn how to read so I brought you every book I could find and spent every moment making sure you got the gist.”

My heart pounded. “Foster, you’re scaring me.”

“I don’t mean to.”

“Then why are you telling me things I already know?” I paused. “No other person in the world but me understands the sacrifices you’ve made for me.”

“There is one thing I didn't shield you from, Emma.” He touched my leg softly and I stood. He walked closer to the flowers and suddenly they didn’t seem as bright. “And that’s the need for money. In my opinion there is no greater love. There could never be.”

I moved closer. “Foster, are you breaking up with me?”

“We were never really together.”

I squinted. “So...so you were never going to marry me?”

He turned around and I could see splotches of red take up real estate on his face. “Marry you.”

“Yes. You promised if I ever was free that you would.”

“Emma, I could never marry a nigger. *Ever.*”

I stumbled backwards, my body flopping in the hard chair. My nose burned and I could feel my intestines bubbling. "A...a...nigger."

"I didn't mean it that way but you need to know the truth. If you stay here, if I continue to hide you, I could lose my stake in the family fortune. And you're beautiful, Emma, just not worth the weight of gold."

"But...all of the things...all of the..." I was losing my breath.

Why couldn't I breathe?

"I would've never made those promises to you at Xavier Estates if I'd known you would've actually left. I was just trying to give you hope. I guess I underestimated my power to strengthen you." He cleared his throat. "What I'm trying to say, Emma is this. You were never supposed to get out. You were supposed to be happy with the life given to you, like your mother. And brothers."

I could barely see him as tears rolled down my cheeks. My temples throbbed and I thought I was about to fall over except I was sitting down. "You never loved me?"

"Have I ever said the words?" He paused. "Have I ever returned the love you gave me when you told me how you felt? Think hard, Emma." He shoved his finger against his temple twice. "You'll find the answer is no."

"Emma!" My mother yelled from behind.

I wiped my tears and turned around to face her. "What, mother?"

"Mrs. Xavier is here and she has men with her. I think they're coming to take us back."

I rotated my head quickly in Foster's direction. "You...you called her?"

"I can't be a part of this, Emma. You're getting in the way of my future. I hope you understand."

My family and I were seated in an extended Escalade. One man, stocky and black, was in the front passenger seat as another equally threatening looking man drove. Behind them were Mrs. Xavier and my mother sitting across from her. My brothers and me were in the back, Clayton's huge body taking up most of the room.

"You were the first you know," Mrs. Xavier said.

"The first what?"

"To escape." She smiled. "I just can't believe you brought Foster into all of this." She sighed. "You are insolent, Zoe and I should deal with you accordingly."

When I gazed at my mother I was surprised that she wasn't crying. I wasn't sure but something about her looked changed. "I just want to protect my family, Mrs. Xavier. Like you want to protect yours."

Mrs. Xavier laughed. "You know nothing about what it means to protect a family. You've had the benefit of my grace since the day you were born." She turned around and looked at us. "You and your children. But you couldn't have *really* loved them and made such a foolish move."

"With all due respect, Mrs. Xavier—I may not know your version of what it means to care for a family but I know what love is. And my love is the reason we're still together."

"Until now," Mrs. Xavier snapped. "And tell me something, Zoe, what pray tell would you have done to take care of your family? Huh? Outside of cleaning you have no real skill set. What have you done in all of your life that deserves the merit of what being a mother brings?"

My mother was quiet and looked out of the window because I knew she'd already lost this battle. It was in the way her chin dropped to her chest and the way she fiddled with her fingernails. Still, her voice seemed calm and measured, despite her chest rising and falling rapidly. "You hate me, Mrs. Xavier." My mother looked at her. "Don't you?"

"What's obvious needs no confirmation."

My mother nodded. "Jealousy eats at your core and will kill your marriage long before I do," she said.

Mrs. Xavier laughed. "Zoe, pray every night that you never love a man so much that it corrupts your common sense. That it erodes the very thing that makes you passionate and a woman. Whether I'm jealous or not is speculative. But when you love as hard as I do you will trade anything for it, even your own children if need be."

My mother frowned. "I will never choose a man over my children."

She laughed. "Then you haven't loved hard enough. And if you had power you would not know what to do with it."

"I would never treat people the way you treat me and the others." She said. "Never."

Mrs. Xavier laughed. "Then let's pray you never get the chance to eat your words."

My mother smiled. "You would have given anything to have sold me off long ago?"

"Of course."

"Then why didn't you?" My mother asked softly.

"Zoe, you know nothing."

"On second thought, I do have a skill and it has been very useful."

"Oh really?" Mrs. Xavier grinned.

"Yes, I possess Mr. Xavier's support and I developed the *skill set* to keep my family together. No other servant was able to keep their children but me." She raised her chin slightly and I saw her reach in her pocket from the left side. It was out of view of Mrs. Xavier and I wondered what she was doing. "I don't have money. I don't even know how to read. But when it comes to persuasion I am a master. And Mr. Xavier is my victim." She paused. "And I'm here to tell you that me and my children will never be what you want us to be again."

My brothers and me gasped at my mother's cold words. She had never spoken this way and I was starting to wonder if the meek woman she showed us at the Estates was all a façade.

Mrs. Xavier's face was strawberry red and she was trembling. "You black, nigger."

My mother nodded and said, "Yes, ma'am. These days I am that but so much more."

Mrs. Xavier looked out the front windshield. "Maxwell, pull over at that bus depot ahead."

I glanced out of the window and saw a Greyhound bus station. We were somewhere in Dallas. When the vehicle stopped I looked at Mrs. Xavier.

What was happening?

Were we going back or not? It didn't matter because with Foster out of my life I had no direction. Even at the moment his words left me sick, unable to feel like myself.

Mrs. Xavier looked at my mother. "I want you and them children of yours away from my husband. If you come back for help, for money, or anything, I will have you all killed." An evil smile covered her face. "You may know how to make my husband *feel*, or even what to do to him not to sell you off but you have no idea what line of work we're in. If you had one idea you would've chosen your words a bit more wisely." She paused. "Now get the fuck out of my vehicle."

My mother opened the door and Clayton and Tristan rushed past me to the exit. My mother followed as I moved slowly.

The moment my feet hit the curb the truck pulled off and my mother vomited on the ground. I saw the handle of a knife sticking out of her pocket she was grabbing earlier and wondered how she would've used the weapon.

"You okay, ma?" Tristan asked rubbing her back. His wild curly fro falling over one side of his face.

She nodded and wiped her mouth with the back of her hand. "Yes. I'm...I'm fine."

As we stood on the curb in front of the Greyhound station I looked at my mother. "Now what? What are we supposed to do?"

She looked around and I could tell she was clueless. "I don't know, but I promise you, all of you, that I will do everything in my power to keep us together." She looked at me, Tristan and then Clayton. "I put that on my life."

"Hey sexy, you guys ok? You look like you need a ride?"

When I turned to the voice I saw a handsome man driving a white van with no windows. Judging by his gaze I could tell he was talking to my mother. It wasn't until that time that I realized how beautiful she really was. I guess I never cared to notice before. "How far are you going?" My mother asked.

"Well I can take you almost anywhere in the state of Texas," he said confidently. "But if you in for the long ride my last stop is Baltimore."

CHAPTER EIGHT

BALTIMORE, MARYLAND

ZOE

"I'm From Nowhere That Matters"

I can't believe I was going to kill my children. When Mrs. Xavier took us in that truck I was going to stab each one of them when we got out than to see us separated.

Luckily I didn't have to.

We were exhausted when we finally made it to Morgan's apartment in Baltimore City. The night caught us when we first arrived so I don't remember much outside of pulling myself up the steps to his top floor apartment. My children groaning behind me.

Since it took days for us to arrive from Texas we collapsed on the living room floor in exhaustion. But when I woke up reality hit me.

Morgan's apartment was extremely small. Tinier than our room back at the Xavier's. Did all black people live like this out here? Maybe I was being ungrateful but since living with them I'd come to expect luxury and this wasn't it. My children shouldn't have to go backwards so the plan was doing whatever I needed to put us where we deserved to be.

Amongst the best.

Morgan's two-bedroom apartment was so filthy I saw a brown bug on Tristan's face while he was asleep. I never saw this kind of bug before so I didn't know what to make of it. Scared out of my mind, I knocked it off his cheek and he was so tired he didn't budge.

When I shuffled a little I heard Emma crying in the corner and I crawled over to her. She was sitting down, her knees pushed against her chest. "It'll get better, Emma." I touched her leg. "I'll see to it."

"And how are you gonna do that, mother?" She roughly wiped her tears away, causing a red bruise to run down her face. "I mean have you taken a look around? We stepped down from royalty and into...into." She looked around. "Whatever this is..."

"Give me some time, Emma. You will see that I will work this out."

She laughed. “And how? Like Mrs. Xavier said you don’t have a skill set. And neither does Tristan or Clayton for that matter. In fact I’m the only one out of all of us who can even read.”

“There’s more to life than reading, Emma.”

Her head fell back. “Like what, mother? Fucking Mr. Xavier? Because that won’t help you out here.”

I slapped her so hard her bottom lip bled. Violence was becoming a part of me.

But why?

Overwhelmed with grief I tried to console her but she was too angry to receive me. Instead she pushed me away and stomped toward the bathroom. Slamming the door behind herself.

Her outbreak caused Tristan to awaken. “Is everything okay?” He yawned.

I sighed. Sometimes looking at Tristan made me understand my failures as a mother. If I could’ve done more, just a little, maybe he wouldn’t be this thing that liked sleeping with men.

With Clayton I was able to pair him with Freddie, one of the servants who worked the land. But by the time Tristan was born all the men were either busy with long hours of work or married to other servants. I think most of them resented that I was able to keep my children together while they lost theirs to other owners. So they weren't willing to help me rear him.

"Everything is okay, Tristan. Its just Emma."

"Is there anything I can do, mama?"

"Yeah, just stay out of the way while I work things out."

I took a deep breath, stood up and walked toward Morgan's bedroom. I had to work him over to convince him that having us here was a luxury and not a burden.

When I got to his room I knocked once and walked inside. The smell, just like the rest of the apartment, was disgusting. A cross between raw sewage and skunk. He rolled over in his bed that was piled high with clothing and smiled. "Am I dreaming or is a beautiful woman in my apartment?" He rubbed his eyes.

"You're awake." I grinned. "Unless you want it to be a dream."

He smiled. "Listen, I'm sorry about the condition of my crib. I ain't use to having company and shit. I'm never even here. I just be dropping stuff off in this joint and rolling out." He scratched his belly. "I'll clean it up later."

He seemed to talk always using broken English. It was something I noticed about a few people in the place we now called home. It seemed to be the language of choice and I knew Clayton would fit right in here. Besides, Clayton told me he had a good feeling about this city as it was where the TV show he watched, "The Wire", was set in.

"So what line of work are you into?"

"I sell drugs."

"Oh, yes, like Tylenol and stuff."

He laughed hysterically. "Where did you come from? I know you said Texas but what part?"

I remembered what Celeste said about never revealing my past. "I'm from nowhere that matters."

"Well I fucks with your innocence I'll tell you that." He sat up and motioned for me to come inside. I did but stood in front of him. "So what's the plan? For you and your kids? Don't get me wrong, you free to stash here until you find a spot of your own but we gonna be tight."

A small sense of relief took over. For now I could make sure we would stay together. "For now I'll take you up on your offer."

"But do me a favor, clear the green out of your son's eyes. He can get hurt out here."

I frowned having an idea who he was speaking about. "Which one?"

"The one with the curly hair. He stares too much and in Bmore, niggas don't like to be stared at."

I swallowed the lump in my throat. "Okay…I'll talk to him." I paused. "So is there anything I can help you with?" I lifted my dress because it was time to go to work. "Anything at all?"

He laughed and placed his feet on the floor. "Yeah…come closer." He paused. "On your knees."

I dropped down and placed both of my hands on his thighs when I was in front of him. "You my special secret. Untouched. I can tell." He removed his penis from his pants. "And I'm gonna keep you here. Right here."

He grabbed the back of my head and shoved his dick into my mouth. It was limp at first but he stiffened quickly. He clasped a handful of my hair and pulled my head up and down as he pumped into my throat. He could be as rough as he wanted because I knew how to suck a dick without gagging.

And was trained to go all night.

"You a pro I see." He said. "I like that...a lot." He moaned. "You in Baltimore now, beautiful. It's best I show you how things work instead of somebody else."

He was the tallest person in the room. His chocolate baldhead looked perfect against his neatly shaved face. I've never seen a black man so put together. He wore blue jeans, a black shirt that looked softer than a regular t-shirt and one small gold chain. I could stare at him all day if he allowed me.

"Can I get some help over here?" Morgan asked waking me out of my trance.

Me, Emma, Tristan and Clayton relieved the grocery bags from his hands. It wasn't until that point that I remembered we cleaned Morgan's apartment. "I'm sorry, Morgan." I hustled my bags over to the kitchen.

"This don't even look like your crib," The stranger said looking around. His walk was smooth and controlled.

He smiled. "That's what happens when you find the right one." He winked at me.

I tried to be humble even though I noticed me and my children were placing the food away alone like we did at the Xavier's Estate. It proved even more that I had to get us out of here. I was done with slavery especially if we were forced to live in poverty and filth.

The stranger looked at me and I focused back on the food. A man that attractive scared me. The last thing I needed was to lose focus on my kids and keeping us together.

"You not gonna introduce me to your, girl?" The stranger said.

Morgan shook his head. "My bad." He walked over to me. "This is Zoe, Zoe this is my man Kennard Black."

Kennard extended his hand and shook mine, holding it a few seconds longer. Afterwards he also shook my children's' hands.

"Why would a woman this beautiful be in your house?" He was asking him but looking at me.

Morgan laughed but I could see embarrassment washing over his face. I keyed in closely to the disrespectful way Kennard spoke to Morgan. It made me feel disgusted.

When we lived at the Estates I had direct access to Mr. Xavier, the man in charge, which kept my family together and safe. With me being in an unknown world now I needed access to an alpha male and if Morgan wasn't it he couldn't do a thing for me.

CHAPTER NINE

KENNARD

"Everything Except The Three Bricks You Holding"

Valla, a tall and obese woman with hanging moles on her face stood over Amanita at an African Hair Braiding Shop in Baltimore City, which she owned. Amanita's seven-month-old baby boy sat in a blue and white stroller next to them as Valla spewed hateful words mixed with spit her way.

"Why have your CPH (clients per head) dropped over the last few months? Huh?" She paused. "And don't tell me you don't have repeated clients because the others have increased their profits."

Amanita looked at her co-workers who were cleaning their already immaculate stations in preparation for their customers.

"I'm not sure, Valla, I've tried all I can but nothing seems to work. They don't want the additional services." She paused. "But...but I will try harder."

When the baby cooed Valla looked down at it. "You know, I let you bring this funk ball bastard into my shop for one reason and one reason only."

When the other girls laughed Valla whipped her head toward them, silencing them instantly.

"I let you bring this thing into my shop so you could exceed quota," Valla continued. "Instead I received a reduction in profits and I have to smell shit every fucking hour. Tell me, Amanita, what exactly am I getting out of this?"

"Valla, I'm sorry." Tears streaming down her cheeks. "If you give me one more chance I promise I won't mess up."

"You right, everyone deserves a chance." She slapped her hands together. "But in order for that chance to work I have a plan." She placed one hand on Amanita's shoulder. "Would you like to know what my plan is?"

Amanita, although fearful, nodded her head yes.

Valla gripped the stroller's handlebars and pushed the baby toward the front door. "Valla, that's my baby! Please don't!"

She stopped. "Do you want to question me about this baby or get money?"

Amanita was confused but knew without her job she couldn't take care of herself or her child. For the moment she would endure the most evil woman she'd ever come across in her 19-year-old life. "Yes, ma'am, I want to work here."

Valla nodded and with evil eyes continued to steer the stroller. Once outside she parked the stroller in front of the only window in the salon. Although Amanita could see the stroller she couldn't see her baby's face.

When she was done Valla waddled back inside, wiped the sweat from her face and approached Amanita. "Leave it out there and focus on your job or you'll both find yourselves on the street."

The bells on the door ring as it opened.

"What are you doing now?" Kennard joked walking in. "And why that kid outside?" He pointed at the window with his thumb.

"Pay it no mind."

Suddenly Valla's entire disposition changed upon viewing her younger brother. Valla and Kennard were the only two in their family. Their parents met in prison. Their father was incarcerated for life behind murdering an entire family due to a debt and their mother was a correctional officer. Their secret love affair continued for fifteen years until he told his cellmate about how he felt about her. Out of jealousy the cellmate snitched about their relationship and she was locked up too. Valla and Kennard grew up in foster care until Valla was old enough to get a job and pull Kennard out of the system.

They hadn't seen their parents since.

Valla walked up to her kid brother and hugged him as he lifted her off her feet, which was no easy task, before planting a kiss on her moist, rough cheek. The mood in the shop was always lighter when Kennard was around and the braiders loved him because with him Valla was happy.

They both walked into her immaculate office where not a stitch was out of place. Kennard plopped in the chair in front of her desk while she walked behind it and sat down. "What you need?" Valla asked.

He laughed. "What makes you think I need something?"

"I know all of your looks. There's the, *'I'm coming to see you look'*, the *'I haven't heard from you in a minute are you okay look'*, and then there's *this* look." She pointed at him. "So what you need?"

"Nothing, V, really." He adjusted in his seat and clasped his hands in front of him. "Just came by because I was in the area."

"Well what's up with that little knotty hair gal you was fucking? She still in the picture?"

He sighed. "Gina moved out last night. Didn't even bother to tell me either. At first I was fucked up because I just bought her that Camaro she wanted but when I went to Morgan's house today I found out the real reason she wasn't in the picture. I needed my slate clean."

"What made her bounce?"

"I think it had something to do with me telling her it was over." He ran his hands down his thighs. "After you put me on that she was fucking the other Kennard Black."

Valla laughed. "I still cannot believe that there's a red nigga out in the world with the exact same name as yours." She paused. "The only difference is his light skin and that he's more vicious and crazy as shit."

"And that's why he's going to find himself dead."

Valla tilted her head. "Well...I'm waiting on what you were about to tell me before we started talking about all this? Something about your slate being clean."

"Oh, yeah. I met this chick at Morgan's crib."

She laughed heartedly. "What is it with you and women?"

He leaned in. "You mean outside of me being a man?"

"I mean outside of you being horny. You like to fuck so much you almost tried to get at me once."

His face flushed with embarrassment. "That's a lie. I told you I was sleep and thought you were somebody else," he said truthfully. "Nobody told you to get in my bed in the middle of the night."

"You only had one air conditioner in your apartment and it was in your room," she said rolling her eyes. "You knew I got put out and needed a place to stay. Could've given me the bed."

He shook his head. "You right, but you came a long way." He looked around. "Ten years later and you make more paper than me."

"That's because your loyalty is the death of your business." She paused. "So what's up with profits?"

"Morgan made a pick up from Texas the other day."

Her eyes widened. "You mean to tell me that he drove the product back himself? What he trying to do? Get locked up forever."

Kennard shrugged. "He made the route not me."

She shook her head. "Kennard, I love you. I tell you that so much I don't think you need hearing it anymore, but the dope game is not your speed." She paused. "As long as Morgan's in your camp anyway. He's too greedy." She sat back in her seat. "You're gonna have to find something else that works for you because he will always be a liability. That move could've landed him in jail."

"He'd rather die than go to prison. Told me himself." He paused. "I'm sure he played it smart the whole drive."

"Smart and Morgan aren't in the same category." She sat back. "I want that nigga—"

His cell phone rang and he held out one finger before answering, halting her words. "What up, man?"

"They got us," Morgan said on the phone. "They stuck us hard, man."

Heart pumping, Kennard stood up and walked to the other side of the office. "Fuck you mean?"

"It was the New York niggas. After I delivered the first shipment they heard we were carrying more and robbed Gasper and his crew. I know you fucked up but at this point I don't know what else to do."

"How much they take?"

"Everything except the three bricks you holding." He sighed. "Fuck! I went all the way to Texas and don't have shit to show for it 'cept a house full of yellow niggas. What I'm gonna do with that?"

Kennard hung up on Morgan because he was feeling murderous. He stuffed the phone in his pocket and paced in place. His lips tight and his eyebrows drawn closely together.

"Let me guess...he told you he was robbed. And you believe him." She shook her head softly from left to right. "I know you don't want to hear this because I've told you many times before but that nigga ain't your friend. He put a few thousand in the pot for that package but it was our money that got the discount for the weight. He ain't out of no real paper, Kennard."

"You know I'm gonna pay you back, Valla." He flopped in the chair.

"It ain't about paying me back and you know that. I don't give no cash out to you I don't expect to lose. You family. Which is why outside of you can't nobody get shit from me." She pointed at him. "Now I'm telling you...that nigga's foul. The only question is what you gonna do about it?"

CHAPTER TEN

KENNARD

"If You Trust Me, I Got A Few Ideas"

Morgan sat at a small kitchen table with Zoe, Emma, Tristan and Clayton to eat supper. So when Kennard showed up uninvited he felt well within his rights to turn him away.

"Wow, I see the family's all together for dinner," Kennard said stuffing his hands into his pockets. "Looks good, too."

Morgan seemed uneasy causing Kennard to believe Valla. "It's been a long day, was just settling down with the yellows for a while." He was referring to Zoe and her family.

When Kennard looked at Zoe he wasn't surprised to see her eyes were planted on him. There was something pure about her, which sat under a layer of darkness that he wanted to expose.

"I need to talk to you, man," Kennard said firmly. "And it can't wait."

Morgan remained seated, angering him even more. "I don't know what else I can say about that situation." He shrugged. "What's done is done."

Kennard grinned. "I can think of a few things. Seeing as how I'm the one out the most paper."

"Kennard, come on, man, I got people here. If I was at your spot I wouldn't do that shit in front of Gina. Wait...you still with Gina? Because the last I heard you shut her out." He picked up a chicken wing. "You better watch her...she might kill your ass if you keep breaking her heart. That bitch crazy."

Kennard thought it was cute how he brought up his girl in front of Zoe. He figured he must've caught the chemistry brewing between them.

"Sir, maybe you should come back later," Tristan said under his breath. His wild curly hair flopping over his face.

Zoe angrily grabbed Tristan's wrist and yanked him toward her before whispering something in his ear. Although she felt he was overstepping his boundaries Kennard saw a fire in the young man he respected. But Kennard's quick examination of Clayton sparked another emotion. He could sense something sinister in his spirit. Ironically it was the same trait that he saw in Morgan.

"Not for nothing, lil man but this is personal," Kennard said to Tristan. He turned his gaze on Morgan. "Let's move, man. We need to talk now."

"I'm not leaving, Kennard." He picked up his fork and shoved rice in his mouth. "Like I said, I'm eating."

Kennard's jaw twitched as he glared at him. "You know what, I'm gonna leave you to it but I left something in your truck yesterday. Let me get the keys right quick."

His eyes widened. "Man, I don't even know where the keys are. You see I'm about to eat, fam. Why you keep pressing?" He patted his pockets and halfheartedly looked around.

Kennard spotted them in the corner of the couch before he asked. Had the house been nasty as usual he might have overlooked them. But now was not the time to call him on it. He needed to move on to Plan B. "I'ma leave you to your meal. But you mind if I go to the bathroom right quick?" He pointed at it with his thumb.

"Why you gotta ask?" Morgan ran a toothpick through his teeth. "After all, we family."

Kennard winked at Zoe on his way to the bathroom. He was inside for five minutes before he returned, only to notice the keys were gone. He kept his comments to himself. "Aight, man I'm out." Kennard gave him some dap. "I'll get up with you later."

"Not if I get up with you first."

Kennard laughed as he bopped out of the apartment. Once inside his new royal blue Ford F150 pickup truck, he grabbed his cell to make a quick phone call. When it was over he waited.

Five minutes later four men with crowbars and bats nodded at Kennard before doing demolition work on Morgan's truck. They banged, pulled and jimmied his windows until they gained entry. It didn't take long for Gasper, his newest young bull, to return with five bricks of white.

He lied.

Nobody robbed him. Valla was right and Kennard was disappointed but refused to shed a tear.

"Want me to take them to the spot, sir?" Gasper asked.

"Take all but one."

"You got it, boss." He paused. "You need anything else? Want us to handle him?"

Kennard focused on Morgan's living room window, which he could see from his viewpoint. He thought it was hilarious how he had no idea that his life was about to come to an end. "No, I got it from here. Hit me when you get to the spot. Woody gonna let you in, he got the keys."

"Yes, sir." Gasper collected his team and ran from the scene.

Originally Kennard was gonna have his men proceed up the steps and put slugs in him but he held back. Instead of murder, which he felt was too easy; he made another call to an unlikely comrade, courtesy of his sister.

For sport, Valla fucked a DEA agent on the side in secret. Although Kennard never understood what any man would see in his mean, fat and ugly sister, this bond came in handy at times. Valla's relationship remained private to most for two reasons. Number one, Valla's brother, Kennard, was on the government's radar as a possible dealer. And number two because her secret DEA Agent was married.

After contacting his sister he cascaded his pickup down the block. Twenty minutes later he could see the DEA descend upon Morgan's mangled truck and the steps leading to his apartment. There were so many agents out there they took over the entire block.

Kennard waited patiently and minutes later he was rewarded when he saw Morgan being led out in handcuffs. He assumed they must've found the half of brick of cocaine Kennard stuffed in Morgan's toilet tank. The move was foul and he was better than it but he wanted to give the snake his proper punishment. Killing Morgan would've sufficed but he needed him to suffer and what better way than to throw him behind bars where he was afraid to be?

To add insult to injury Kennard pulled out of the parking spot and rode slowly by the cops. When he saw Morgan being handled, Kennard raised his chin to drive home his assault. With his free hand he fired a finger gun in his direction. Morgan shook his head before being stuffed in the police cruiser like a foot inside a sock.

When Kennard drove up the street he didn't go too far. He waited patiently until he was certain the coast was clear. And when it was he ascended the steps leading to Morgan's and knocked. When Zoe opened the door he leaned on the frame. "Your man's not coming back."

"I figured," she said under her breath. She stared at him. "You have anything to do with that?"

"Would it make a difference?"

She looked away.

"So what you gonna do?" he asked as he gazed inside. "And your family?"

She shrugged. "I have no clue right now."

He nodded. "You don't know me and I don't know you. But if you willing to take a shot and trust me, I got a few ideas."

CHAPTER ELEVEN

EMMA

"The Moment I'm Able To Leave I'm Gone"

When Kennard opened the door nothing was inside his house. It looked like the place had never been lived in, except I saw the bottoms of the white walls were scuffed where furniture must've scratched at the paint.

Overwhelmed, I sighed and stood over in the corner while we all stared around.

I didn't want to live here.

The neighborhood looked grimy, nothing like where I lived in Texas. It was as if all hope had been sucked out of the neighborhood and the blacks accepted the fate that they'd never amount to anything. It was in the way they sat on their steps, surrounded by trash that grew in place of the missing splotches of grass. It was in the way they leaned against shiny cars, while people who looked starved roamed around like zombies with their hands out.

What kind of place is this?

And why hadn't Foster told me my people lived this way?

"I can't believe this bitch," Kennard said, rubbing his temples. He walked deeper inside, blinking several times as if everything would magically reappear. "She took everything. All of it."

My mother stepped up to him and whispered, "Is there something I can do to help?"

She's funny.

How can she do anything when she can't even read? The only thing she can do is clean up his place and give him sex like she did my father and Morgan.

Kennard exhaled. "No...I just...I mean..." He rubbed his temples again. "Look, give me a few secs to figure this shit out." He stormed inside a room and slammed the door.

I put my hands on my hips. "Now what, mother?" I asked. "Because now we're worse off than we started."

"Emma, please. Not now."

“Not now what? If he puts us out where we going to go?” I paused. “You should never have disrespected Mrs. Xavier.”

“Emma, ma’s gonna work it out,” Tristan said. He removed a rubber band from his arm and placed his hair in a ponytail on top of his head. “Just give her some time.”

Clayton laughed and yawned directly after. He removed his sweatshirt, balled it up and sat on the floor. “Well, I’m ‘bout to get some rest. When ya’ll figure this shit out wake me up.” He fluffed his shirt up and laid his head on it like a pillow.

I hate him.

“Tristan, I’m not feeling Clayton but I’m frustrated too.” I paused. “Had you stayed with the Xavier’s, Foster would’ve let me live with him. It was because I brought you that he couldn’t help. Everyone knows it’s easier to hide one person than four.”

“That means you didn’t want me to go either?” Tristan asked.

I looked at him and exhaled. I loved Tristan and although I could do without my mother and Clayton, I would’ve been sick if I couldn’t see him. “You know I didn’t mean it that way.”

"Then what did—"

Kennard came back into the living room and walked up to my mother. "I'm sorry about this." He scratched his head. "I wanted to help you guys and didn't anticipate that my ex would take out all the furniture. If you want, I can put you up in a hotel for a few weeks and—"

"But where will you go?" she asked.

He shrugged. "I guess I have to stay here."

My mother approached him. "Me and my family don't bow out when things get rough. You were willing to help us and we want to be there for you. That is if you would have us." She pointed at Clayton who was already snoring. "As you can see we can sleep anywhere."

He sighed. "Okay, I'm gonna take you to my sister's shop and give you my credit card to order some furniture off the net. I don't care how much it costs so—"

I laughed. "Kennard, I don't mean to interrupt but I'll be better suited for this job. My mother can't re—"

"Emma!" Tristan yelled. "What you doing?" He frowned.

I was about to let Kennard know she couldn't read when my brother stopped me. I knew Kennard would find out anyway so for now I would leave it alone.

I cleared my throat. "I mean, mother doesn't like to deal with that kind of stuff. She usually has me do it." I looked at her. "Right, mother?"

She gazed at me, Kennard and then the floor. "Right."

I smiled at Kennard. "See..."

He threw his hands up in the air. "Whatever works. It may take a few weeks but we'll make this crib better than it was before that bitch got me for my furniture." He looked around. "I guarantee it."

One Week Later

Using Valla's computer I was able to get the entire house furnished. There were only three bedrooms so Tristan and Clayton shared one and I had my own since Kennard said a girl needed privacy. Of course Clayton tried to dispute but Kennard held firm and it made me like him more.

Although my mother cooked and cleaned, I was the one who handled the cash Kennard left in the kitchen drawer to care for expenses. She and my brothers did what I said based on the budget and I was proud that I had things running like a machine.

But my heart still hurt.

I missed Foster.

Using the number I held to memory I sat on my bed, pressed the phone against my ear and waited for him to answer. The sounds of the ambulance playing in the background of Baltimore were distracting and I hoped he wouldn't hear it. There was always something happening in this neighborhood and my dream was to get away from it all but I didn't want to without Foster.

After two rings he finally answered. "Hello."

"Foster..."

Silence.

"Foster, please. Talk to me."

"Hey, Emma." He sounded like he wanted to hear from me and I tried to hide my smile.

"I don't mean to bother you, I just, I just wanted you to know that you were on my mind."

A police siren blared outside. "Where are you, Emma? The hood?"

How did he know?

"Yes, it's a run down neighborhood but its temporary." I paused. "I wanted you to know that I thought about what you said...about money being important. And I wanted you to know that one day I will be a woman you will be proud of."

"Emma—"

"Please don't say anything mean, Foster. Even if you don't feel the same way, let me hold on to hope. Let me hold on to the dream the way I use to." Tears rolled down my face. "I'm begging you."

"Take care, Emma."

"You too." When I hung up I grabbed the pillow and cried into it. There was nothing more in this world I wanted but him. And I would not rest until he was mine.

We ran out of food and Kennard asked me to go to the store with Woody, some kid he had running errands for him. Before Kennard let me go with him he was so stern with Woody that I wondered why Woody agreed to take me.

"Let me tell you straight up...this is not some bitch you can toy around with." He was standing outside of the house next to Woody's car. "If I find out you treating her with anything other than respect, disappear yourself."

Woody took it calmly, like he yelled at him all the time and I was intrigued. I wasn't too impressed with him in terms of looks because he looked like the rest of the niggers standing on the block—long cornrows, tattoos on every part of his skin and a long gold chain. But seeing how he dealt with Kennard so calmly made me understand why Kennard trusted him.

"She's good with me, unc. You know that." Woody said as he opened the passenger side door. I slid inside and was even more surprised when Woody closed the door behind me like a gentleman.

Kennard said a few more words outside of the car and seconds later Woody entered. We were halfway to the grocers when I looked over at him and said, “I’m not having sex with Kennard you know? My mother is.”

He shrugged. “Whatever Kennard does in the privacy of his home is Kennard’s business.”

I nodded. “So how you know him?”

“Who, Kennard?”

I laughed. “Who else?”

He shrugged again. “Kennard’s a stand up nigga. He could’ve left the hood a long time ago but he stayed and looked out...know what I’m saying?”

Now I was the one who shrugged. “Not sure if he deserves any award for staying around this dump.” I looked out the window. “Because the moment I’m able to leave I’m gone. Forever.”

He nodded. “You entitled. Just be sure you leave walking and not tucked. The Baltimore life is heavy and has a way of changing people’s directions.”

I laughed. “Entitled huh?”

He looked over at me. “What’s funny?”

“Nothing, I guess I’m surprised you know any big words.”

Now he was the one laughing. “If you think entitled is a big word then you the one who’s funny, not me.”

I rolled my eyes. “Whatever.”

“Listen, just because I run errands for Kennard doesn’t mean you and I have to be friends. I’m a hood nigga and you a stuck up bitch so our worlds don’t have to cross if we don’t let ‘em. So let’s not let ‘em.”

CHAPTER TWELVE

ZOE

"He's Taken"

Dinner was ready and the only thing I needed was the table to be set. But when I looked into the living room I saw Tristan setting things up alone. I told him to have Clayton help so where was he? "Where is your brother?"

Tristan folded the napkin like we use to at the Xavier Estates. "He said he was tired. I think he's still in bed."

"Well where's Emma?" I wiped my hands on the red apron I was wearing.

"She's in the bathroom on the phone."

"Talking to Foster?" I asked.

"You know I can't tell you that, ma."

I rolled my eyes. "It doesn't matter anyway, just as long as she doesn't tell him where we're living."

I sighed and there was a knock at the door. I opened it, forgetting what Kennard said a few days ago. *"Zoe, I'm not sure about the world you lived in before but this here is the hood. You have to be careful before you welcome the unwanted into your home,"* Kennard told me.

But it was too late. And because of it I was staring into the face of a tall light-skin girl with freckles all over her face. From the doorway she looked inside of the house and seemed shocked. "Uh...where is... Kennard?"

"Who are you?" Tristan asked walking up behind me.

"Go finish the table," I told him.

"But, ma. We don't know who—"

"Tristan, go." I pointed.

When he was gone I focused back on the pretty but tall girl in front of me. I wanted to clean up my mess by getting rid of her without my son's help. It's bad enough that Emma's in charge of running the household because I can't read or count money. I didn't want Tristan's help with security. "He isn't home. Who are you?"

"Gina."

I blinked and realized even more I made a mistake. "Did you want me to take a message?"

"You can take a message but it's for you."

I frowned. "Excuse me?"

"I'll excuse you and kick some advice your way too. Kennard is an asshole that'll do whatever he can to ruin your life. If you can deal with that then you're in for a ride but the moment you think he's anything other than a selfish bastard you're in for heartache. From one pretty bitch to another you've been warned."

"Do you still love him?" I asked.

"If I did?" She placed her hands on her hips.

"He's taken, Gina. I need this situation more than you and I'm letting you know now. Stay away from here. Come around again and you can get hurt." I slammed the door in her face.

"Fuck you, bitch!" She yelled banging on the door.

When I heard her stomping away I turned around and Tristan was staring at me. "You okay, ma?"

"Yeah, just finish setting the table."

My thoughts were all over the place and I wasn't sure why. It's not like I'm in love with Kennard because we just met. But if he puts me out my children are homeless and I'm not about to allow that to happen.

Five minutes later Kennard came home and shook his head when he saw the food spread on the table. A huge smile was on his face. "I gotta know something before we go any further." He closed and locked the door.

"What is it?" I asked.

"Is this going to be my life now? Or are you just trying to win me over?" He laughed. "Because I don't want to get use to this shit if it ain't real."

"Every night this is for you. If you want it, Kennard. All you have to do is say the word."

He smiled and rubbed his chin. "You know I want this. What man wouldn't?"

"Then consider it done."

He winked at me and I grinned. Kennard had a style about himself that I was falling for and if he kept it up I could see myself being with him. But Gina's words rang in the back of my mind and made me unsure if I could trust him.

When Kennard was finished with me Tristan walked up and gave him a handshake, followed by Emma. He was about to sit down when he looked around. "Where's Clayton?"

"Sleep again," Emma said shaking her head. She took a seat.

"Well tell him to get up." Kennard demanded. "Your mother cooked and we should respect her by eating together."

Wow. I've been cooking all my life, for as long as I could reach the stove and that was the first time I heard those words.

"I did tell him," Emma said. "But he told me to tell ma to bring him a plate to his room. And that he was sleepy."

"This kid..." Kennard shook his head and walked toward Clayton's bedroom. My heart rocked because this was a fragile moment. One wrongdoing by Clayton could get us evicted. I didn't breathe until a minute later when Kennard returned with Clayton who rubbed his eyes and flopped down in the chair. He wasn't wearing a t-shirt and his muscles popped.

I guess he was mad and not trying to show it.

"Let me say something to you all," Kennard addressed the children. "During dinner time everyone helps and everyone is expected to sit at this table." he pointed at it. "Your mother's cooking is a luxury, not an entitlement." He paused. "I never got a home cooked meal from my moms because she wasn't around. So, if you got a mother who here for you, you need to respect that."

"I feel the same way when I go grocery shopping and no one helps me," Emma said.

"Aye, Emma, I'm not talking about you right now." Kennard was stern. "Like I said, dinner time belongs to your mother and it will be the one time she always gets respect. I promise you that."

Dinner was a hit and now Kennard, his sister and me were sitting in the living room talking. The children were in their rooms and part of me felt like I should've gone with them like when the Xavier's ate and entertained when I was a slave. But things were different now and I had to constantly remind myself.

They kept offering me wine but I refused, afraid of what I might say or do. Whenever Mrs. Xavier drank she looked so nasty that I never wanted to come off like her. The thing was he persisted and I decided to give it a try. Besides, I wanted to loosen up because we didn't talk much since I always felt guarded. The most he knew was that my family and me were homeless after living in Texas and he respected my privacy.

Three Glasses Of Wine Later...

Everything was blurry and suddenly I wasn't worried about a thing. I felt empowered and even friendlier.

"Looks like she's relaxed now," Valla said pouring herself another glass. "Now I can see why you like her so much. Outside of her being a beautiful and all."

Kennard looked at me and smiled. "Yeah, haven't seen her like this ever." He rubbed my leg. "But she was cool without the sauce too. Just wanted her to kick back a little that's all."

"I feel like...I feel like...fucking." I said out loud, the words rolled off my tongue.

Where did that come from? Guess I wanted him in this way for so long that it just popped out.

They both laughed. “I think she’s saying she wants you in the bedroom, Kennard,” Valla laughed and her stomach jiggled. “Can you handle that?”

He looked at me and didn’t seem as excited as she was. I hoped I didn’t make a mistake by drinking. “You okay, Zoe?”

“I’m fine,” I nodded. “Really.”

“So tell me, what is a beautiful woman like you doing in Baltimore with your kids alone?” Valla asked. “I mean you all cook, clean and obviously keeping my brother happy. I just gotta know more.”

Still feeling the alcohol I said, “I was born a slave...with my kids...and we wanted...we wanted...to be free and to stay together.” Their eyes widened.

Kennard placed his wine glass down and moved closer. He positioned his body so that he was looking into my eyes. His hands were clasped in front of him and his gaze was intense. “Zoe, did you just say that you were a slave?”

I remembered what Celeste said about not revealing my past but now it was too late. "It's a long story."

Valla stood up and shoved Kennard out the way with her hips so she could be closer. "Tell me what it was like being a slave."

I sobered up quick and gave the worse recollections of my memory. How after 24 hours of giving birth to my own children, I had to cook dinner for the Xavier family. Details rolled out that I hadn't known I remembered maybe cause I wanted to forget. The alcohol in my system even caused me to talk about how my daughter was raped while I hid in a closet.

When I was done I wanted to go to bed instead Valla said, "So the Xavier's had a house full of people working for free?" Her eyes seemed to glisten as the pain of my past ripped at my core.

I knew immediately she didn't care.

"Valla, what's wrong with you?" Kennard asked. "My folks just said she was forced to do all kinds of crazy shit and you stepping to her about free work?"

She stood up and her eyes seemed to twinkle. "Kennard, I have to go. I'll explain everything later." She ran out of the house.

Kennard's arms were wrapped behind my neck, his warm breath caressing my forehead. I had sex many times but this was my first experience at intimacy. I felt a genuine connection with him. It was like he wanted to save me. Like what I shared about my life as a slave brought us closer.

"What do you want, Zoe?" Kennard asked. The room was dark but I could see the glistening whites of his eyes staring. "I want to make it my goal to do that for you. No matter what it is."

I looked up at him. I've never been asked that before and I felt ashamed for not having an immediate answer. Life never allowed me to dream for anything other than keeping my family together. "I don't know."

"Think hard...nothing is out of the question."

"But why?"

He exhaled and rubbed my cheek with his finger. "You've never had a life. I mean, I know you fucked old boy but that shit was wrong. You were raped too and I want you to see that all niggas not like them people. I want you to know that some men are real and I want to prove it to myself too."

My heart pumped wildly inside my chest. "Well, I want my family to stay together and to be protected." I paused. "I want to have the relief I never felt by knowing that no matter what, we won't be ripped apart. I want my daughter to be safe and my sons to grow into strong men. I want peace of mind, Kennard. Can you give me all those things?"

"You're safe with me, Zoe. You and your family. I've made a lot of promises that I didn't keep in the past but for some reason I want things to be different for you. For us."

I swallowed. "Gina came by earlier," I blurted out. "Before dinner."

He sat up and turned the lamp on next to his bedside. His body seemed rigid, not soft like before. "Hold up...she did what?"

I sat up and positioned myself so that I can look at him. My legs folded in front of me Yoga style. "She came over looking for you." I paused. "Why did you guys break up?"

"My sister found out she was fucking around on me. I just bought her a car before Valla told me that shit." He shook his head. "I knew it was over but she bounced without a word." He paused. "Hold up, you let her in my house?"

Embarrassed I held my head down. "No, but I did open the door."

He slapped his hand against his forehead. "Zoe, you have to be careful in Baltimore." His voice was loud but I got the impression that he was worried for me instead of himself. "Never open that door for someone you don't recognize. We not going to be here forever, but for now we live in the hood amongst some of the worst kind. If you want me to keep you safe you have to listen. You have to obey." He paused. "Do you understand?"

I nodded. "I'm sorry, Kennard."

"Don't be." He sighed. "That bitch gonna make me choke her out though. Popping up over my crib and shit." He said to himself. "That's on everything." When his cell phone rang he answered. "Valla, what's up? I'm talking to Zoe."

His eyes widened and he was pulled into the call. "Yeah I got a passport." He paused. "Where we going?" He looked at me and then away again. "Africa?" He said confusedly. "For what?"

CHAPTER THIRTEEN

EMMA

ONE MONTH LATER

"Don't Say Shit Else To Me"

Foster's eyes were bluer than I remembered. As I lie on top of him I inhaled the scent of his skin, afraid it would be a long time before I saw him again. He ran his warm hand down my back; the hotel sheets under us were dampened with our sweat. I prayed for this moment and today I was in heaven. "Thank you for seeing me, Foster." I whispered. "I know you didn't want to and it means a lot."

He kissed my forehead. "You don't have to thank me."

His voice made my body tingle.

"But you know I have to get back to DC," He continued. "Uncle Porter would kill me if he knew I left the convention or that I was with you."

I felt heavy. "I never asked before but what does your family do?"

He sighed. "We deal mostly in real estate but I have a feeling other things go on too that they don't let me in on."

I nodded. "But I thought you wanted to open your own business after you finished college? Why change?"

"The family needed me so I did what I must." He paused and kissed me again. "Now you have to get dressed and leave, Emma. Quit stalling."

I felt sick to my stomach and for a second I looked down at his suitcase wishing I could stuff myself inside. I would be his slave a million days over if it meant we could be together. Like he promised. Instead I stood up and got dressed as he requested.

When I was done he walked me to the door and closed it behind me without another word. It was easy for him to let go. I was having all of the trouble. As I walked down the hallway every nerve in my body pulsated. I left him feeling heavy, like my limbs were stuffed with led. If this was all he could give me I would have to take it but I needed more.

I was halfway to the lobby when my stomach churned, forcing me to rush into the bathroom before I vomited on myself. Hovered over a toilet I regurgitated everything I ate that morning which wasn't much.

When I finally made it to the lobby about twenty minutes later I saw Foster at the check out counter. Needing to see him once more I walked up to him to say goodbye. When I tapped his shoulder he turned around and frowned when he saw me. "I just wanted to say goodbye once more."

He looked over my head and around the lobby. Finally his evil eyes rested on me. "I'm sorry, who are you?

I laughed, thinking he was joking. "Foster...are you serious?"

He chuckled hard. "I don't know who you are but I know you better get out of my face." He cleared his throat.

My stomach churned and I couldn't move. My feet were planted even though I wanted nothing more than to run. And then I felt a warm arm around me and a wet kiss on my cheek. "There you go, shawty. I been looking all ova for that ass."

I blinked a few times and looked to my left. I was staring into Woody's kind eyes. And if you can believe me they were the sweetest things I'd seen in that moment.

"Who you thought this was, bae?" Woody asked pointing at Foster. "Our driver?"

Foster's face went from anger to confusion and although I was devastated, I think I saw a hint of jealousy too.

"I...I was..." My words wouldn't exit.

"Don't worry about it, wifey," Woody continued. "Our driver's outside. Now let's bounce, we have places to be and people to see." He frowned at Foster and walked me out of the hotel.

It wasn't until I was in the car that I could finally breathe. I cried so hard at the betrayal Foster exhibited that my lower abdomen felt like I'd been doing sit-ups all week.

Woody didn't say anything, just maneuvered the car down the road. Like he didn't just help me maintain some dignity in the hotel lobby.

When I finished crying I looked over at him and said, "I didn't need your help you know."

He laughed. "Yeah, aight."

His cool attitude while my world was tumbling down made me want to hurt him. “I should tell Kennard what you did just now by kissing me but I’m not.”

He shrugged. “If that’s the thanks I get for helping you then I deserve everything that’s coming my way.”

I frowned. “You don’t care about anything do you?”

He looked over at me. “Look, you the one who had me sitting outside in the car for two hours while you fucked a white boy upstairs. If that’s what you into that’s your thing and I’m not gonna stop you.” He shrugged. “But to snitch because I saved you from looking stupid is low key mean.”

I frowned. “I wasn’t looking stupid.”

“You looked dumb as fuck.”

I crossed my arms over my chest. “You know what, don’t say shit else to me, nigger.”

He winked. “I like it like that, ma. As a matter of fact let’s do that shit forever. You don’t say a word to me and I won’t say a word to you.”

We drove in silence thick with tension for the next twenty minutes. When we pulled up in front of my house he parked and looked ahead. "I'm not going to tell Kennard," I said.

He laughed, still not looking at me. "Is that your way of saying thank you?"

I frowned. "You know what...fuck off." I pushed open the door and stormed out and he immediately pulled off. Tires screeching down the road.

When I made it inside of the house I was happy to see Kennard was back from Africa. But when I gazed at my family I knew immediately something was wrong. "Come inside, Emma, I have to talk to you about something." Kennard said standing next to the table.

I sat down, along with my mother and brothers who were already present. "What's going on?"

He sighed. "I want to be honest with you guys because what I'm about to say may offend you." He walked toward the corner and leaned against the wall.

He was putting us out.

I was certain.

"The way I use to get money is on hold right now. Morgan's trying to stop my cash flow from prison and he's doing a good job. Without saying too much I'm under pressure from the law but I found a temporary way to hold us over that I'm not proud about."

Maybe he wasn't putting us out.

"Whatever it is we support you," Tristan said.

"Yo, shut the fuck up and let the man talk," Clayton yelled.

I rolled my eyes at him. Since when did he start saying *'yo'*?

"Come on, boys," mother said. "Let's hear Kennard out."

Kennard nodded. "To make a long story short Valla found someone who knows how to bring undocumented workers from Africa to America. And while we were there she was able to bring this help to work in her braiding shop. Their names are Fashna, Maganda, Issa, Lumo, Serwa, Tano, Ori and Kessie. You'll be seeing a lot of them in the future."

"But why so glum, Kennard?" I asked.

"With them Valla stands to make a lot of money but she wants my help." He paused. "If I do it, it won't be forever." He paused. "And I won't do it now if anybody in this room has a problem with it."

Now I had to know because the look on my mother's face told me she was already aware. "I don't get it, Kennard," I said. "Why would we oppose you using braiders for your sister's shop? Undocumented or not?"

He cleared his throat. "Because the women who are coming won't have the freedom her old braiders did. They will be...they will be...slaves."

CHAPTER FOURTEEN

ZOE

SIX MONTHS LATER

"The Only Thing I'm Worried About Is Family"

The Braiding Salon was packed.

Valla fired all her paid braiders the moment she brought in the workers from Africa. She couldn't have them in the shop with her undocumented girls. Business was booming. Three braiders were busy working on clients and three other braiders were in the back prepping for upcoming appointments. Emma was in the front taking payments and Clayton was at the apartment across the street with the other two girls.

Valla told me repeatedly that the girls were not my friends and that I should treat them like commodity but I could never see the business that way. I understood what it meant to be forced into labor and if she wanted my help she would have to follow my rules. Although I was in charge I felt like I was their friend not their boss and the girls respected me.

I was in a good mood because I finally had the letter Celeste gave me read. She told me that chances are because of my upbringing that I may have deep-seated anger and to find ways now on how to stay grounded. But I wasn't like her. I was a woman who was making a difference and I loved who I was becoming.

When I saw Maganda bent over holding her stomach, I rushed up to her and placed my hand softly on her back. "What's wrong?"

"It's my stomach," she said with tears in her light brown eyes. Skin the color of melted chocolate she was one of the prettiest girls I'd ever seen in my life. "I think I'm getting period," she said with a deep African accent. Initially it was difficult to understand the girls, since they all spoke little English, but now I was getting use to their dialect.

"Are you in pain? Do you need some Tylenol or something?"

She nodded. “I think it’s worse. I may have to lie down. I’m so sorry, Zoe. Please don’t be mad at me. I get cramps bad and—”

“Don’t worry about it, Maganda.” I grabbed her hand and squeezed lightly. “Really. The other girls can handle your clients. We’ll be fine.”

I remembered the days I worked for the Xavier’s and would be in so much discomfort in my knees that they would swell up like balloons. But Mrs. Xavier didn’t care. I was forced to continue my shift until all of my responsibilities were done. I was determined that I wouldn’t do my girls that way no matter what Valla said. It was bad enough she forced them to work from 7:00 am to midnight most days.

Didn’t they deserve rest while sick?

I reached into my pocket and handed her the keys. “Here, run across the street, take some Tylenol and grab a nap. If Clayton gives you a problem tell him I sent you and to give me a call.”

“Are you sure, ma’am?” She asked, fright all in her eyes. “Because I don’t want trouble with Valla.”

“I’m positive. In fifteen minutes you should be as good as new.” I looked over her head. “Kessie, come here and finish Maganda’s client.”

The customer looked up at me and said, “Ah, ahn! I don’t want nobody else doing my hair. Why she can’t finish what she started?”

“Don’t worry...Kessie is the best in the shop.” I touched her shoulder. “Trust me.”

Maganda hugged me and rushed out the door just as her client settled down. It felt good that I had the power to make sure my girls were safe and treated fairly. If only I had someone like me at the Xavier’s Estates maybe things wouldn’t have been so bad.

With her handled I walked up to Emma to redirect Maganda’s clients. She was plaiting one of her French braids as usual. “I sent Maganda to the apartment to catch a nap. Give all her clients to Kessie.”

She frowned, her jaw dropped. “Valla’s not going to like that, mother. You shouldn’t have done it.”

I crossed my arms over my chest. “Well I don’t care what she likes. I’m not about to let one of our workers braid hair while in pain.” I paused.

"And since your cycle is as bad as mine I would think you'd understand."

She rolled her eyes and erased Maganda's appointments, moving them to other girls' schedules. "This is not going to end well."

I frowned. "Emma, the only thing I'm worried about is family. As long as the girls are making quota Valla's not going to care so relax."

I continued to make sure the shop was running properly while Valla was away. Not only was Valla's Braiding Salon profitable, the money was enough for Kennard to move us to a better home in Upper Marlboro Maryland. Add to that the fact that our relationship bloomed and in my eyes I was living a dream.

I knew Kennard didn't like what we had to do to make money so I wanted the girls as comfortable as possible, hoping that would put him at ease. And as far as I could tell it did.

The shop was busy and it wasn't until four hours later that I remembered Maganda hadn't returned. We were doing well without her so it wasn't a big deal. But I called the apartment on the shop's phone to make sure she was okay. The line rung repeatedly and kept going to voicemail.

Clayton was in charge of watching the girls who weren't scheduled today so where was he?

It took three more times of me hanging up and calling back to get Clayton to answer. When I heard his voice he sounded like he'd been asleep. His laziness was disgusting. "Clayton, you know you're not supposed to sleep while watching the girls."

"Sorry, ma." He yawned. "I'm up now though. What's up?" He coughed.

I walked toward the back of the shop and sat in the chair. "How is Maganda doing?"

"Maganda?" he said. "How would I know? Ain't she there with you?"

"What do you mean how would you know? I sent her home because she wasn't feeling well."

"Alone?" He asked.

My heart dropped. Normally Clayton escorted the girls from home to work but I believed Maganda because she'd been so trustworthy. Only to realize I may have made a mistake. "Clayton, go ask Issa and Ori if they'd seen Maganda."

"Okay..."

The phone went silent. As he put me on hold my stomach churned. If I lost Maganda there would be a huge dent in profits and our lifestyle because she was good and quick. Five minutes later Clayton returned. “Ma…I don’t see Maganda. I don’t see the other girls either.”

My eyes widened. “What…why not?” I yelled. “Where were you?”

“I’m sleep in Fashna’s room and they were in the living room the last time I saw them.”

“But what about the door? It’s locked from the inside and you’re the only one with the key.”

“I guess somebody else had one too because I still got mine.”

Oh wait.

I shook my head because I gave the other key to Maganda.

I totally forgot.

Me, Valla, Kennard and Tristan were sitting at the dining room table. Emma was at the apartment across from the shop sitting with the other girls and Clayton was on his way with Woody to pick her up. Trusting Maganda caused us an estimated one hundred thousand dollars reduction and Valla was pissed.

To make matters worse she wrote a letter and left it in the apartment before freeing herself, Issa and Ori. It read:

You people are nefarious. And I hope you rot in hell.

– We Are No Longer Your Slaves, Maganda.

After Emma read the letter I tried to conceal my hurt. I trusted Maganda and treated her like family because I would've wanted someone to do the same for my children and me. But now I was made to look like a fool.

"Your mistake cost us big, Zoe." Valla's fingers were clasped in front of her on the table. She was beyond angry with me.

"I'm sorry. She was in pain and—

"You don't get to make decisions. Especially if your decisions costs us. Your mistake is the reason they must live in this house. Plus you have the space." She paused. "Being in the city gives them too many resources for help. But out here…"

"Valla, I don't know about this shit," Kennard said standing up. "When we agreed to help you I never said I would have this shit in my home." He pointed at her. "Now Zoe made a mistake but she's not a monster. Neither am I."

"So I'm a monster because I'm doing what's needed to take care of all of us?" Valla asked.

"You black, Valla." He sighed. "You black and you enslaving other black people. Don't you see anything wrong with that shit? Fuck is wrong with you?"

Valla's nostrils flared. "If it hadn't been us it would've been someone else." She paused as she waved her hand. "Now I know you don't want them here but look at your beautiful home, Kennard! The business that you hate has given you back your lifestyle. You should be sucking my largest toe."

"You don't deserve an award. You went and picked women from their homeland and made them slaves! And now you want them in my basement?"

Valla stood up and approached him. "You're my brother and I love you but your girl is into me for a lot of money. Now you know what I do to people who are into me for a lot of money. Are you willing to work with me or not?"

"Are you threatening my woman?" He yelled.

"You know I don't make threats, brother." She squinted and walked over to the table. "You couldn't make money in the drug business if your life depended on it. Thanks to Morgan, in prison singing like a baby bird, you need this business. Fuck you goin' do...get a job? You need me."

"I can't do this," I said. "I'm not about to treat people badly just because we need them to make money for us. I won't."

"Not even if it was to feed your family?" She asked him.

I looked down at my hands. "I'm not this person," I said. "I can't be evil just because we're making money." I paused. "How do we know they won't escape and go to the police?"

"Did you go to the police when you were a slave?" Valla paused. "You said it yourself that you stood by and watched your own daughter get raped. And you did nothing."

I rushed over to her with my fist balled. I wanted to hit her so much my hands moved on their own. "Never talk to me about that moment again. Ever."

"Sit...the...fuck...down." She said through clenched teeth. When I was seated she cleared her throat. "We have a business and those girls are commodity. Treat them like that and you will stay focused. Treat them any other way and you'll have a problem I'm not willing to pay for."

"Valla, just let it go," Kennard said. "Zoe's never gonna see things your way."

"She will," Valla smiled. "I can see it in her eyes. She wants power just...like...me. And soon who she really is will be revealed."

When Kennard's cell phone rang he answered. "Hello."

He paused and his eyes widened. Immediately he looked sick and I wondered who was on the other line. I walked up to him just as he hung up and placed the cell back in his pocket. "What's wrong, Kennard?"

"Baby, sit down."

"I don't want to sit down." I paused. "What's wrong?"

"It's Woody...he called to tell me...to tell us that...that...Emma is dead."

CHAPTER FIFTEEN

SERWA

ONE HOUR EARLIER

"Are We Going To Fight"

Fashna stood in the corner of the room, her face flushed red. Serwa, and the other girls surrounded her and listened attentively. Although a descendent of Africa, like the others, her skin was light due to her mother marrying a white man resulting in her being born. Like the other girls she came to the country under false pretenses.

"You'll be able to live the American dream," Valla promised Fashna. *"You'll have money, your own home and a future. All you have to do is come with us. And bring some girls. Surely you don't want to deprive them of this great opportunity do you?"*

Of course she didn't. So Fashna told her cousin and friends of the wonderful opportunity waiting for them in the US. It took much convincing but in the end her cousin Maganda, Lumo, Serwa, Tano, Kessie, Issa and Ori followed her to the land of dreams.

Fashna, like the others, was excited as they boarded the plane to America. But the moment they landed their passports were snatched along with their hopes and dreams. Since most of them knew very little English they were strangers in a big world and it was Maganda who pushed off and escaped. Stronger than the others mentally she would rather roam the strange country in freedom than submit to slavery. She wanted the others to come with her but they were too afraid.

Until now.

"We can't really be talking about doing this," Fashna said in her native African tongue. "Can we?" She was hysterical and on the verge of an emotional breakdown.

Serwa walked calmly over to Fashna and wiped Fashna's long hair out of her vanilla colored face. "If we stay this will be our lifestyle. Forever. Do you want to stay in a place that doesn't respect you? That doesn't love you? We are descendants of kings, Fashna. And yet we're slaves."

"But I don't want to hurt anyone, Serwa," Fashna cried. "Can you honestly say that you do?"

Serwa released her and ran a hand down her own head. She kept her hair in a low cut that looked regal against her mahogany skin. "What I know is this...I cannot be this *thing*, Fashna. I can't be a slave. We are better than this." She looked at the girls. "All of us. And the only thing standing in the way of our freedom is that girl...in that room." She pointed at the door.

Lumo, the most violent out of the group looked at the women with wild eyes. Her family was murdered by a guerilla group leaving her alone in Uganda. Her life was over until Fashna convinced her to go to Africa because she had no direction. She was ready to do whatever her friends were to escape but she didn't want to do it alone. "She's right. We must move." She pointed at the floor.

"But how?" Fashna asked.

"We are in a big city," Serwa whispered. "Someone is bound to help us but we have to move now because I believe they are going to relocate us in a few days. To a place not so busy as this city."

"But how can we be sure that the Americans will help once we escape?" Fashna asked.

"We have to maintain hope, my sister. Thinking about *what if* won't do us any good if we don't make a move now." Serwa paused. "So"— she took a deep breath— "are we doing this as a group? As a family?" She looked in all of their eyes. "Are we going to fight for our freedom and think about where we will live later?" She paused. "Or will we let down our pride and roll over and die?" When they all nodded yes Serwa took a deep breath. "So, let us remember the plan."

"We have it," Lumo said. "Let's go."

Serwa smiled and cleared her throat. And in the loudest voice she could muster she yelled, "Emma!" She paused. "Come! Fashna!"

As planned Fashna lay on the floor and held her stomach and within seconds Emma entered the bedroom with her hands on her hips. Unlike Zoe, Emma loved ruling the women because it made her feel powerful. "What now?" She asked full of attitude.

Serwa tried to think of the English words to explain herself. "Sick...Fashna." She pointed down to her.

Emma walked further into the room, creating a path in the middle of the girls. Once upon Fashna she stared down at her. She didn't believe she was sick at all. Laughing she asked, "So what happened? Because sick or not Valla is not letting nobody else stay home from work tomorrow." She smirked. "Maganda messed that up for all you bitches."

Serwa and the others didn't understand everything Emma said but they did gather that Maganda's recent actions put Valla and the others on high alert.

"She sick," Serwa said again. "Please help."

The moment Emma bent down Lumo hit her with a lamp. But instead of falling to the floor Emma hit her head on the side of the dresser, a gash six inches deep tore at the flesh of her forehead.

She was killed instantly.

Blood gushed from the wound and the moment she was down Serwa went at her pockets in search of the key.

"Where is it?" She asked in her native tongue. "The key, it isn't here." She was frantic and before long Emma was naked on the floor as they all tried to find it. Serwa stood up and with wide eyes said, "It isn't here."

Lumo ran out of the room and searched the living room. It took fifteen minutes but the key was nowhere to be found. They had no idea that after Maganda escaped that Valla decided to be the only one with the key until the girls were relocated. Even Emma had to wait for someone to open the heavy bolted door to let her out of the apartment.

Lumo returned. "It's not here." Her breaths were heavy. "She doesn't have the key."

Serwa and the other girls tore the apartment up only to discover that Lumo was correct.

Fashna's face reddened. "We've made our situation worse, Serwa. And it's all your fault. The Americans will kill us now."

Serwa walked over to the bed and flopped down. Taking a deep breath she threw her face into her hands. She never saw this scenario happening. Emma not having the key was not even a possibility, after all why would they lock her inside? Didn't they realize the girls were dangerous? And willing to do anything to escape?

"We have to get our stories together," Serwa said seriously. "We have to convince them that this was an accident. Because if they don't believe us we will not survive this. None of us."

PART TWO

CHAPTER SIXTEEN

KENNARD

ONE YEAR LATER

"You Did What You Had To Do"

"I got it anyway and you're gonna take it whether you want to or not," Kennard said as he walked to his car with a white prescription bag clutched in his free hand. When he reached the car he ended the call and tossed his cell in the small compartment by the steering wheel. Tristan was in the passenger seat waiting on him.

When he arrived, Tristan immediately noticed Kennard's stiff demeanor and said, "Sir, is everything okay?" He removed a rubber band from his arm and tamed his wild curly hair.

Kennard sighed. "Your mother's getting worse, son. We have to keep an eye on her."

Tristan nodded and leaned back. "I wish there was something I could do. It's like she hates everything now. Mainly me. I don't recognize her."

Kennard sighed. “Let me handle your mother, son. I don’t want extra pressure on you. Don’t worry, I have it under control.”

Since Emma was murdered Zoe’s life spiraled out of control. After hearing the news that her only daughter was killed she suffered a stroke, which rendered the right side of her face in a permanent slump. Although the girls said it was an accident and Valla believed them, Zoe wasn’t too convinced. And to get back at the girls Zoe tortured them in ways most would consider unimaginable.

She had become evil.

Kennard felt the pressure of her new mood but it was Tristan who did his best to make things easier. As horrible as she acted he was in love...still.

Tristan cooked when Zoe didn’t. He cleaned when Zoe couldn’t and he expressed his love to her on a repeated basis. But nothing worked. She moved as if she hated him.

Out of Zoe’s sons, Kennard liked him the most. His decision was easy to understand. Clayton was lazy and untrustworthy and Zoe allowed it. With losing Emma she was determined that nothing would happen to him. But with Tristan she didn't seem to care about his fate.

Kennard pulled into traffic. "I just want you to know that what you're seeing, with the girls in the basement ain't the way shit is supposed to be." He looked over at him and gazed back at the highway. "You understand that don't you?" He paused. "Treating people that way is wrong, son."

"I understand, sir." He nodded. "I really do."

Kennard shook his head in disgust thinking about the slavery. "I fucked up by letting my sister rope us into this shit but I have a few things in the works. So it's just a matter of time."

"Anything I can do, sir?"

Kennard sighed again. "What is your mother's thing with you? There's a disconnection that I'm not understanding. You can talk to me, son. I'm willing to listen."

Tristan knew if he wanted to have a serious relationship with him he would have to tell him that he had been with boys, even though he was not acting on the urge anymore. The saddest part was that the urge grew stronger as the months went by. He was trying to be the man Zoe wanted hoping he could win her love.

For the first time he was going to reveal his sexuality to Kennard in the hopes that he could help him. But before he could speak the car suddenly stopped and both Kennard and Tristan's bodies jerked forward. Angry, Kennard brought down his fist on his horn and beeped at the two flamboyant gay men walking in the middle of the street while the light was green.

"I can't believe this shit!" He yelled rolling down the window. "GET THE FUCK OUT THE STREET, FAGGY MOTHAFUCKAS!"

The gay men looked at him, struck a pose and busted out laughing before walking away. This did nothing but anger Kennard even more. Tristan on the other hand felt devastated. He knew in that moment he could never tell Kennard about his secret.

Ever.

Thirty minutes later they arrived at a run down house in Washington, D.C., Kennard parked and looked ahead.

"I gotta go in right quick to check this dude about my money. I'll be back." He eased out and disappeared into the house.

Tristan sat silently and waited for his return.

He was just about to turn on the radio when he saw someone sneaking along the side of the house. The man was hooded and dressed in all black and when the stranger peered into the house's window, and removed a silver gun from his waist, Tristan knew he had to think quickly.

Kennard didn't say whom he was meeting but Tristan knew this was off. He was about to call him on his cell until he glanced down and saw that it was still in the car.

Heart rocking and blood pressure pumping, he looked around for something he could use as a weapon. He was only sixteen and had never been in a situation like this but it was time to act. He cared about Kennard and didn't want to see anything happen to him.

When he looked in the back of the car he saw a silver bat resting on the floor. He grabbed it and moved quietly out of the car. Tristan was so afraid a little urine released from his penis and dampened his jeans.

Slowly he entered the yard and crept behind the man who was obviously trying to get inside. The man's back was faced him so he didn't see him coming. When he was close enough Tristan raised the bat and slammed it across the back of the man's head. His scalp opened slightly and released a stream of red slick blood.

"What the fuck," the man yelled, his eyes wide as tires. Realizing a kid was whooping his ass; he blinked a few times and snatched the bat. In possession of the weapon he brought it down on Tristan's right arm, immediately breaking his index finger. They wrestled with one another and everything seemed to move quickly when Tristan heard gunfire sound off inside of the house.

What was going on now?

Tristan was too afraid to ask questions about where the sound originated. Or if Kennard was safe. In fight or flight mode he scuffled with the medium sized man until he snatched the bat back. Using his good hand, he hit the man once more over his shoulder causing him to drop to the ground. Tristan wasn't done with his attack. While he was low Tristan pounded him repeatedly in the forehead until the pink flesh pushed from his brown skin like wet cauliflower. Although the man was not moving he was about to hit him again until he was lifted off his feet from behind.

Ready to finish him off, he was about to attack until he saw it was Kennard. Quickly he rushed him toward the car, pushing him safely inside.

Kennard snatched the bat out of his hand, threw it in the backseat along with a grey duffle bag and jumped into the car. Behind the steering wheel he removed a gun from his waist and fled the scene.

He drove fifteen minutes and when he reached a desolate area he parked and tried to catch his breath. Besides, he just murdered the man inside the crib who owed him money, before robbing him of everything he was due and a little more. Had he not been so angry he would've thought clearly and saw the set up coming from miles away with the stranger outside of the house trying to gain entry. Luckily he didn't have to because Tristan had his back.

Kennard clasped the steering wheel and looked out into the street. "The man…who you were beating…was trying to get inside wasn't he?"

Tristan, trembling, nodded his head.

Kennard exhaled. "So you saved my life."

Silence.

Kennard wiped his hand down his face. "We can never tell your mother about what happened here today." He faced him. "She can never know about this because all she'll do is worry. And with Emma gone I need her not to worry. You got it?"

His eyes widened. "Yes, sir."

"Good...good..." he sighed again. "You gonna go through some things over the next few days. I went through the motions too when I first killed a man. But I want you to know that it wasn't your fault. You did what you had to do and I will always remember that."

Tristan's eyes widened. "So he...so he's dead?"

"Yes, Tristan."

"And you killed someone in the house?"

"Yes." He paused. "And like I said we can never talk about this again."

Tristan's stomach contents bubbled. It wasn't until that moment that he was aware of what he'd done. All he wanted was to help Kennard, the man who showed him unconditional love.

And now he was a murderer.

Feeling like he was about to explode he pushed the passenger side door opened and vomited onto the grungy street. From inside

Kennard placed one hand on his back, the other gripping at the steering wheel.

CHAPTER SEVENTEEN

ZOE

"Keep An Eye On Tristan"

They're (Fashna, Lumo, Serwa, Tano and Kessie) standing in a cage I had built inside the basement.

Just...for...them.

I only allowed them out when it was time to work or sleep but only if Clayton is watching them. I don't trust any of them.

These whores killed my daughter.

I'm certain.

Completely naked, they're arm and arm, no room to sit or lie down without falling on top of each other. Every time I look at them I feel hate brewing inside of me, like coffee in a pot because I knew they had something to do with my daughter dying and it's my life's work to make them pay.

Slowly and horribly.

I sat in my chair across from them and drank a glass of wine. "You whores smell like shit. But you probably like it that way."

When I glanced to the right I saw Fashna standing in the corner, doubled over, clutching her stomach. I knew the bitch was probably faking sick and I wasn't about to buy it.

Not this time.

Serwa stepped forward and wrapped her hands around the bars. Blood puddles thick with clots were on the floor where she stood because she was on her period and I refused to give her tampons. She swallowed and in broken English said, "Please, ma'am. Fashna." She gazed over at her. "She's sick."

I crossed my legs. "You mean to tell me that you're on your period and you're thinking about her?" I paused. "I would think you'd ask for something to stuff that rank pussy of yours instead."

I scratched the side of my face that drooped downward after my stroke. Nothing about myself was the same. I looked like a monster.

"Ma'am...I think she is...in trouble." Serwa swallowed and took a deep breath. I knew she was trying to pick the right words in English and I loved every minute of it. "She...may...die."

I looked at Fashna again and rolled my eyes. "If she dies let her. After losing Emma I could give a fuck about any of you."

I felt tears welling up remembering my daughter and I took a deep breath. After my daughter died I begged them to tell me who was responsible. Even offered to let them out but no one talked. They stuck together and because of it all will suffer.

"You're an evil, ugly bitch," Lumo said in a deep man-ish voice. "I'm so glad that stroke wiped away your beauty and presented the world with the monster you really are." She paused. "And one day, very soon, you will rot in a hell made especially for you."

I laughed. "So I see you're getting even better with your English."

She smiled, her dark eyes looking directly into mine. "Yes. I learned every vile word necessary to express my hate." She laughed. "How am I doing?"

I chuckled harder and sipped more wine. "Are you dumb or suicidal?" I sat my wine glass down. "I have your life in my hands, Lumo." I showed her my palms and clutched them into fists. "Do you want me to squeeze the breath out of you? And your friends?"

"Stop it, Lumo!" Tano yelled. "Don't antag...antag..."

"It's antagonize and shut the fuck up, Tano," Lumo barked. She focused back on me. "Before I die, I will feel your throbbing veins beneath my fingertips as I squeeze your throat. I promise." She stuck out her tongue, licked her lips and gripped her pussy. Pushing her index finger inside of her vagina she sucked off the cream. "I'm horny just thinking about it."

I stood up. "For your insubordination none of you bitches will eat. And you have Lumo to thank."

I stomped upstairs just as Kennard and Tristan entered the house. Both of them looked beat down and I wondered what happened out there. I know Tristan was probably sexually attracted to my man, seeing as how he was a fuck boy and all and I will deal with him appropriately soon.

Very soon.

"Hey, ma," he said holding his hand.

"Hey, Tristan." I crossed my arms over my chest. "Your plate is in the fridge if you're hungry."

"I'm okay...thanks anyway," he said in a low voice.

"What happened to your hand?"

He looked at Kennard. "Nothing, ma. I'm fine."

"Go to your room, son," Kennard said placing a hand on Tristan's shoulder. "I'll see you tomorrow."

When he disappeared upstairs I wrestled in my mind what to say about this relationship he was building with Tristan. I decided that bringing it up now would not be the best moment. Something else was wrong and I didn't know what. It was all in his eyes. "You look exhausted. Can I get you anything?"

"I'm good, just gonna take a shower."

"Can I join you?"

"Actually I want to be alone for a few ticks."

Disappointed, I stepped away from him and moved toward the wall. "Since my looks washed out and my stroke came you don't want to touch me anymore. Its so evident."

His eyes widened. "Zoe, you can't be serious."

I crossed my arms tighter across my chest. "Well that's how I feel."

He grabbed me by the waist, looked me in the eyes and kissed me passionately. "I want you to see me and feel what I'm about to say. There is not a thing about your body that I don't love, Zoe. A thing. You are my everything. Why would I love you less because of a disfigurement caused by losing your child? I ain't no creep."

A tear rolled down my cheek and he vanished it with his thumb. "I don't know I just...I just feel so different, Kennard."

"That's on you not me."

"I know. It's just that every day I feel myself swelling up with more and more hate. And I want it off of me but I can't shake it." I clutched my fists. "My daughter's gone and she was tortured her entire life for me." The veins in my face pulsated.

"Give it some time, Zoe." He rubbed my back. "And I think when the women leave after I get this money then that'll help too."

"I know they were involved, Kennard."

"You don't know anything for sure, Zoe." He frowned. "If you did I would kill them myself." He paused and lifted my chin so that we were eye to eye. "Let that shit go, baby. It will kill you if you let it and I don't want that for us. Please."

He asked me to join him after all.

My back was pressed against the warm shower wall while Kennard held me up, his dick deep inside my body. My breasts pressed against his chest as we kissed passionately.

His hands gripped at my cheeks and spread them apart as he pounded into me like a mad man. My body vibrated but this wasn't about me. It was about reminding Kennard that although I wasn't physically the same woman, I could fuck him harder.

Ugly face and all.

And when we were done he called my name.

Afterwards we lay in the bed and I figured now was the time to tell him what was on my mind. "Do you know about Tristan?"

He shifted a little and placed his hand on my thigh. "Know what about Tristan?" He yawned.

"That he's gay."

His eyes opened and he sat up in bed like a bug was on the comforter. "What the fuck do you mean?"

"Kennard, Tristan is into men. And as much time as you spend with him you can't tell me that you aren't aware of this. You're probably giving him the wrong impression as we speak."

He frowned. "Hold up, are you questioning my sexuality?" he placed his hand on his chest. His eyes evil.

"No...it's him...I mean...you spend so much time with him."

Kennard got out of bed and scratched his head. He looked blown away.

"What's wrong?" I asked.

"It's just that I said some things today...in the car. And if it's true that he's gay I know it's tearing him apart." He paused. "Fuck."

"So you really don't know?"

"Zoe, I had no idea about Tristan. But even if I did, it wouldn't change the love I have for the kid. He's up and up, way different than Clayton."

I frowned. "So you don't love Clayton?"

"I'm not saying that. It's just that you protect him too much. Tristan is the one who needs your love. All he wants is to be there for you. Maybe you should give him a break."

"So I'm not a good mother?" My brows lowered. "Is that what he's been telling you?" Tears rolled down my cheeks and I didn't realize I was that hurt until that moment. "We've been through too much, Kennard. Please don't call me a bad—"

"Zoe, stop..."

"But you're taking his side and—"

"Zoe, let it—"

"You need to listen to me, Kennard." I interrupted. "I love Tristan but if he wants you I will let him go."

His eyes widened and he looked at me as if he didn't know me. As if I were a stranger. "When we first got together you said you would do anything to keep your family together. That statement alone made me beat for you. So you telling me that's changed?"

I trembled and placed my fingers over my mouth. I never spoke that way and still I couldn't shake the fact that it was true. Maybe Mrs. Xavier was right about love after all. "No...I...I mean...I'm just under so much pressure."

He sat on the bed and leaned against the head post. "You have to be careful of how you treat him, Zoe. He's more fragile now than you realize."

"Why? What happened?"

"It doesn't matter. Know that he's changed forever and he needs his mother's love. Your rejection at this point in his life can turn him into a monster." He paused. "Is that what you want?"

My stomach flipped.

"Kennard, I'm willing to try harder with Tristan." I paused not believing my own self. "Please forget what I said...I'm just...overwhelmed."

"Well I need you to be strong, especially while we have those girls in this house. Tristan told me that Serwa said Clayton might be raping them. Clayton can't handle them by himself and to be honest I don't trust him."

I frowned. "Clayton didn't rape anyone," I advised. "Those whores throw themselves at him." I pointed at the door. "Because he's in charge."

He grabbed one of my hands. "You sound stupid and I'm not trying to hear all that. I don't want him alone with the girls, am I clear?"

I looked down. "Yes, Kennard."

"I'm working hard on my end, Zoe. I'm getting back into the game because the shit my sister's into ain't for us." He paused. "But the moves I'm going to make are gonna require time." He paused. "So that means you have to treat the braiders with care. I don't know what goes on in that basement but I'm trusting that you are being fair. Please."

Silence.

"I need some air," I scooted off the bed until my feet were on the floor.

"I understand, bae. I'm gonna get some rest too. It's been a long day." He laid down and pulled the sheets over his head.

He didn't give a fuck about me. All he cared about was Tristan. Nobody understood how I felt about losing Emma. The guilt weighed down heavy on me. I went out on our deck and looked out at the acres of land before me. It was nothing as big as the Xavier Estates but it was home and it was mine.

Life was different now.

CLAYTON

Fashna pleaded with Clayton to be gentle but he carried on as a complete asshole and didn't give a fuck. The power he received by being in charge over women who were vulnerable caused him repeated hard on's and he wanted her to submit like the slave she was.

With the other women faking sleep, he forced his penis into her mouth until she choked. And when he couldn't cum because the bile in her throat from gagging stung his dick he flipped her over on the flat mattress and rammed into her anus.

He was vicious and careless.

He plied into her buttocks until they both were saturated with blood and semen. Only when he was done did he rise before creeping up the steps.

ZOE

When it got too chilly on the deck I walked back inside and moved toward the basement but on my way I saw Clayton locking the basement door with his key and it was almost two in the morning. "Clayton..."

He jumped and when he turned around I saw his pants unbuttoned and belt hanging open. "Ma...I...I..."

I put my hands up. "I don't care what you do, just don't get any of them pregnant." His eyes widened as if he didn't believe what I was saying.

"For real?"

"Yes...and do me a favor...keep an eye on Tristan." I pointed at him. "I don't trust him around the girls."

"You got it, ma."

I crossed my arms over my chest. "When you were downstairs, how was Fashna?"

He scratched his baldhead. "On second thought, I don't remember seeing her."

"Tomorrow pull her out of the basement. Don't let her go to work. I don't want her infecting the others if she has something."

"You...you think she sick?"

"I'm not sure but I don't want the others getting ill when we need this money."

He cleared his throat and wiped his forehead. "Where you want me to put her?"

"I'll think of a place for that trash later."

CHAPTER EIGHTEEN

TRISTAN

"Stay The Fuck Away From Me"

Tristan crept down the stairs of the basement holding a bag. When he reached the bottom step he saw the girls were lying on their bunks sleep. Soft snores filled the air. The odor was so powerful it almost knocked him over.

Why you doing this shit, man? He thought to himself. *Leave these girls alone.*

He shook his head and moved past the women until he spotted Serwa's short boy haircut. When he found her he bent down and gently touched her arm. "Serwa."

She popped up afraid she was in danger until she saw Tristan's kind eyes peering at her. A peaceful calm and smile spread across her face. Over the months they developed a close bond. He saw strength in her and helped her as best he could. No one knew about their relationship but the girls and he wanted to keep it that way.

“I have some food and the girl stuff you asked for. You know...for your pussy.” He handed her the bag filled with bread rolls, butter and tampons.

Serwa didn’t understand everything he said but his eyes told her he cared and was sympathetic to her plight in life. And in her predicament that was enough.

She looked in the bag. “Thank you.” She gripped his hand and a tear rolled down her face. “Thank you.”

“No problem,” he smiled. “Make sure you hide the female stuff and tell your friends to eat everything tonight. I don’t want my moms seeing this shit. She’ll know it was me and she already hates me enough.” He was about to bounce when she grabbed him by the forearm.

She swallowed and searched her mind for the right words. When she realized she needed help expressing herself she shoved Lumo who was next to her asleep. Lumo yawned and in Serwa’s native language she asked Lumo to translate.

Lumo listened to her attentively in African and said, “Serwa says Fashna was taken earlier. She wants to know if she's okay because she wasn't well before she left."

Tristan seemed confused. "What do you mean taken?"

"She was very ill," Lumo continued. "We don't know what was wrong with her but she was doubled over in pain. And a little while ago Clayton came and took her. We're afraid he may kill her because he raped her first."

Tristan scratched his head and backed up. "I...I can't get involved in all that."

"But you're already involved," Lumo said with lowered brows. "You know in your heart what your mother is doing is wrong. We need you to help us." She pointed at him.

"Help you what? Leave?" He asked harshly. "I can't do that shit. This is my family."

"But your family is evil, Tristan." Lumo responded, no longer using Serwa's words to communicate. "And if you stand by and let this happen you're just as guilty. And if you're guilty I won't let anybody stand in our way when we have to leave. Even if I have to walk over your dead body."

Irritated for having his kindness not appreciated he was about to walk away when Serwa grabbed his hand with his broken finger. "I will suck you off." She gripped his penis. "I'm willing to do anything, Tristan. Just help us...please." Her English was clear that time.

He pushed her back. "Stay the fuck away from me." He looked at Lumo. "Both of you bitches."

He ran up the steps.

When Tristan bopped upstairs he was headed to his room when he heard a knock at the front door. He walked toward it and looked out the peephole. When he saw Valla's face he started to say fuck her because she wasn't his favorite person. That is until he considered the day he and Kennard had with the murders. Reluctantly he opened the door and blocked her entry. "What up, Valla."

She tried to push inside. "Move, boy."

"Everybody's sleep." He extended his hand, shoving her back outside like a nigga. "Can I help you?"

"I swear you fuckers are so rude around here. Where is my brother?" She peered inside.

"He's sleep."

"Well why weren't all the girls at the shop today? I lost a lot of money and it's putting me in a bad mood."

He shrugged. "You gotta ask my mother all that. It's not my place."

She lowered her brows. "Well you tell her that all of my girls better be at the shop tomorrow." She rolled her eyes. "If I knew she was gonna stop them from coming to work I wouldn't have let them stay here."

"You want me to tell her you want them moved to your spot? Because I'm sure it won't be a problem."

She cleared her throat. "Don't be a cunt. Just give her my message, smart ass." She stormed away.

CHAPTER NINETEEN

SERWA

"We...Want...Fashna"

In a huddle, inside the basement, Serwa spoke seriously to the girls in their native tongue. "It's been two weeks," She whispered harshly. "Two whole weeks since we've seen Fashna and I know something is wrong."

"You know my question is always the same," Lumo said. "What's the plan and when we making a move? Because if you ask me we do too much talking. How many times could we have strangled Zoe with our bare hands and we let that ugly bitch get away? How many more offenses are we to endure before we fight?"

Serwa looked at all of them. "I say we refuse to work until they show us where Fashna is. And when we're sure she's okay we leave. But not without her."

Lumo laughed. "Are you crazy? I would rather we run than to do something so dumb. These people will kill us if they can't get their money."

"Have you ever seen a gun? Ever?" Serwa continued. "And outside of Clayton's threats with knives while he's raping us I doubt he has a gun either."

"I don't know, this sounds so dangerous," Tano said.

"Oh, Hush, Tano!" Serwa snapped. "You only say these things because you're a pet. You love having sex with Clayton and you're jealous he chooses Fashna over you. Tell the truth...we all know it."

"That's not true. I want to go home, back to Africa."

"I can't tell because when Clayton picks you, you seem none too happier to fulfill his wishes."

"It's true," Kessie said who was normally silent.

"It's not!" Tano yelled. "The only people I'm loyal to are the ones in this room. If there's a plan I'm with it, just tell me what it is."

When the light came on they all dropped to their beds and faked sleep. "I heard voices down here," Zoe said sternly. "What's going on?"

Silence.

“So this is how you’re doing it?” Zoe asked with her hands on her hips, her hair in a tight bun that sat on the top of her head, making her appear more intimidating.

Finally Serwa rolled over and rubbed her eyes. She sat up and said, “We...want... Fashna.”

Zoe crossed her arms over her chest. “And why do you want her?”

“We’ve...been...worried...for friend.”

“Worry about the work tomorrow instead, bitch,” Zoe said harshly. “The numbers have been slacking lately and we won’t stand for much more.”

“You mean like your face?” Lumo said.

“I’m serious.”

Serwa’s eyebrows rose. “But we...work more...harder...increased profit.”

Zoe’s brows lowered. “What do you know about profit? You don’t know shit about it outside of what I tell you.” She pointed at her.

Silence.

“Now get back to sleep and don’t let me hear you goofing off again down here.” She stomped up the stairs and slammed the door.

Serwa waited for a minute before speaking again. "Until we see Fashna, work drops off. Does everyone agree?"

Each girl whispered, 'I', in the darkness and Serwa smiled.

"Good...we're going to get that bitch now."

CHAPTER TWENTY

FASHNA

"Tell Me The Truth"

Fashna was diagnosed with Rheumatic fever and at first Zoe didn't know what to do with her. Her condition caused her to have a high fever, achy joints, sore throat, swollen lymph nodes, vomiting and a rash. Outside of a few meds the nurse requested that she rested. At first the nurse wanted to know who she was but when Kennard told her she was a friend of the family and paid her handsomely she dropped the subject and remained silent.

When she was gone Zoe watched her grip at her stomach and moan. Had the nurse said she was well and faking Zoe planned to do unimaginable things to her flesh.

Turned out the child was sick for real.

When Fashna rolled over she was startled to see Zoe leaning against the wall staring at her. She tried to sit up in the bed but every part of her body ached. "Ms. Zoe. Can I...do something...for you?"

Zoe moved closer to the bed. "What happened that night, Fashna?"

Fashna groaned and said, "I'm sorry...I don't understand—"

"Stop fucking playing with me." Zoe's hands were clenched in tight knots that hung at her sides. "What happened to my daughter?" When Fashna remained silent Zoe sat on the edge of the bed. "You know the saddest part of all this? I like you, Fashna. Always have. I even need someone to help me out with the girls. That means privileges. And that person could be you but I need you to tell me the truth. Which means no basement."

Fashna's body trembled.

"What happened to my daughter?"

"I don't know, Ms. —"

Zoe pressed a blade against the vein in her neck. "Was it you? Did you kill my daughter?"

Fashna remained still and Zoe pressed the sharpest point of the blade deeper into her flesh, pricking her lightly. A tiny trail of blood oozed down her neck and fell at the crease of her breasts. “I’m not gonna ask you again. Did you kill my—”

“Ms. Xavier, we have the—” Woody stopped short when he saw Zoe over Fashna’s sickly body.

When she saw him she stood up and hid the knife behind her back. “What are you doing in my house, Woody? Where’s Kennard?”

He looked at Fashna and then Zoe. “Uh...I got the money Kennard told me to drop off.” He pointed at the door with his thumb. “It’s down stairs. Want me to bring it up?” He looked at Fashna again who looked as if she’d seen a ghost.

She nodded. “Oh...no...let me handle that right quick.” She looked at Fashna once more and walked out.

Woody followed Zoe. His mind on the girl with the bloody neck.

Fashna was still sick, but Clayton was as selfish as usual. He forced her on her knees, on the hardwood floor. Once down he made her suck his penis as he urinated in her throat. Her body was weak and she could barely stay straight but her health was not of his concern.

"Open wider," he said sternly looking down at her. "If I don't cum I'm going to kill you. Do you understand me, slave?"

She nodded.

She opened wider and he bit his lip as he oozed with pleasure, gripped her hair and pushed and pulled until his semen spilled out of her mouth. When he was done he wiped his dick off on her sheet and said, "You almost made me fuck you up by moving slowly." He pointed at her. "Be glad I got mine off." He clutched his crotch.

When he left the room he ran into Tristan who was standing at the door. "What you looking at, faggy?" Clayton said.

Tristan glared at him, upon overhearing what happened in the room. He was starting to develop a deep-seated hatred for his brother that he couldn't explain. "One day you gonna pay for what you doing to that girl. It ain't part of the job and you gonna see what it feels like to be—"

"Get the fuck out my face, nigga." Clayton pushed him out of his path and proceeded to his room.

CHAPTER TWENTY-ONE

WOODY

"So You Questioning My Loyalty"

Woody eased in the car with Tristan who was in the passenger seat waiting to be taken to their next stop. They were on their way to meet Kennard who was at the trap house. Woody was trying to focus on upcoming business ventures but after seeing Zoe standing over Fashna's body a few days back he was confused and concerned. He barely knew what was happening in the house as is, or where the girls who left the braiding shop each night slept.

But now his conscious was eating at him.

What the fuck was wrong with ugly as Zoe?

"I told you, you should've taken the money in your crib that day instead of me," Woody said with an attitude.

"I didn't feel like it," Tristan responded turning on the radio. "Plus Kennard gave you the paper not me. If a dollar was missing you'd be responsible."

Woody shook his head. "Well I saw your moms when I was there." He merged onto the highway. "And it kind of fucked me up."

Tristan looked over at him. "She lives there." He shrugged. "Why that fuck you up?" He removed a rubber band from his arm and pulled his braids together behind is head forming a ponytail.

Woody cleared his throat. "Yeah, well, I saw her with the red shawty that work at the braiding shop. The chick was in the bed and your mother was over top of her looking all creepy and shit. My eyes never been the greatest but she looked like she had a knife against her throat. Stabbing at shawty and shit."

Tristan adjusted in his seat. "Leave it alone, man."

Now Woody was really interested. Tristan maintained his calm.

"What's happening in there? I know the girls working for pennies because my mother from Ghana and I know a little of the dialect when they be rapping. But what I don't understand is why she had a knife and what really happened to Emma?"

"Emma fell and hit her head," Tristan sighed. "That's how she died. I told you that."

"But it never sat right with me."

Tristan shook his head in irritation. "Pull over up the block." He pointed ahead.

Woody frowned. "Why? We gotta meet—"

"Pull the fuck over!" Tristan yelled.

Woody followed suit although he felt like breaking the boy's jaw. After all, it was the first time he came at him in such a pointed manner. When he parked Tristan adjusted himself so that he could address him eye to eye. "What goes on in that house is family business. My family." He pointed at himself. "And if you want to continue to have the relationship you do I suggest you stop asking questions."

Woody's brows lowered. "So you questioning my loyalty?"

"Are you a part of this family or not?"

Woody sat back in his seat and looked ahead. "Yeah, man."

"Then don't talk to me about the girls or what goes on in my crib. Aight?"

"Aight, man, whatever." Woody pulled back into traffic.

CHAPTER TWENTY-TWO

ZOE

"It's Time To Earn That Back"

I walked down the steps with Clayton following me with a trash bag full of sandwiches and chips. Rat food. That's what I fed them. It had been four days since they'd eaten and I starved them so long that Valla was popping up over the house regularly asking a billion questions about their weakness.

When I walked downstairs Clayton tossed the food on the floor. They all moved toward it until I raised my hand. "Don't move any closer."

They paused.

"I'm feeding you today but make no mistake, I will remove food again if I find that any one of you are causing trouble in my home or the shop. Am I understood?" I looked at Serwa and Lumo who stared at the others and then back at me.

"Okay," Serwa said in a low voice. Her face dressed in a scowl.

"Before you eat I need to make something else clear." I clasped my hands in front of me, the way Mrs. Xavier use to do. "The quota has been raised because of the slack over the last few days. You are now required to earn $6,000 a week. Per girl."

The women moaned.

"I don't know why ya'll tripping," Clayton said. "Ya'll mothafuckas been faking sick for a month. It's time to earn that back." He clapped his hands together and then rubbed them briskly.

"Ms. Zoe..." Serwa said softly. "We can barely make quota now."

I noticed her English was a little better and figured Lumo had been working with her.

"Maybe in the future you'll think about that before you decide to go against me," I said. "This is a product of your ungratefulness. Luckily for you I don't hold grudges long. But I will expect each one of you to earn your keep or else things will get worse." I paused. "Do you understand?"

"Yes, ma'am," Tano said smiling at me, before looking at Clayton who winked at her. "We understand."

I clapped my hands together. "Good, now eat up. And tomorrow it's back to business."

They fell on top of their food like dogs.

When we made it upstairs I walked into my room and told Clayton to follow. "What's up, ma?" He leaned against the wall.

"Later on today bring Tano upstairs and warm up to her a little." She paused. "I need her eyes and ears with the girls. Fashna is almost better and we can use her later but for now I need Tano under my fingers."

He raised his eyebrows. "What you mean warm up to her?"

"Just what I said. I don't trust them bitches, especially Serwa. And I want eyes on them at all times."

Clayton pouted. "Don't know why you so worried about Serwa. Lumo the one always talking shit."

"Oddly enough I respect that about her because at least I know where she's coming from."

"If I do that do I get to keep Fashna upstairs?" He paused "Permanently?"

"I have allowed Fashna to stay up here as long as I did because you begged. Even though she has to work at the shop like the rest. But I don't want you falling for this girl if I grant your wish. Am I clear?"

He shrugged and stuffed his hands into his pocket. "Yeah, ma."

Kennard and Tristan came in the house. No matter what he did Tristan was always at his side and I was growing irritated. Not only were they close but I noticed that Tristan kept extra cash on him at all times and his hair was always neatly braided and I don't think he wore the same pair of shoes twice in a week. Clayton got new clothes too but it was clear who was being spoiled.

And guess what?

It wasn't me.

"Aye, Kennard, you gonna take me with you next time?" Clayton asked with a smile. "I'm ready to help you out if you'll have me."

Kennard cleared his throat. "Man, you not trying to be on the streets. It's not glamorous work." Kennard looked at Tristan. "Plus your mother needs you with the girls."

"Well I don't want to be with the girls. I want to help you."

"Maybe next time," Kennard said.

"You know what, fuck it then. Forget I even asked." He stormed away.

"What's up with Clayton?" Kennard asked Zoe.

"Let's not even get into it." I rubbed my eyes and looked at both of them. "But what's up with you two?"

Kennard smiled and touched Tristan on the back. "Show her, man." He handed Tristan his cell phone and I sat on the bed.

Tristan turned the phone on and read, "Today president...president..."

"Presidential," Kennard said helping him. "That's a big word, man. It's okay you didn't get it. Take it easy and remember the things I taught you."

Tristan looked at him and smiled before focusing on the phone again. "Today presidential hopefuls met with seve...seva...several community leaders about...about the issues."

"That's enough, man." Kennard gave him a handshake and he seemed proud. "Good job." He looked at me. "Ain't it, baby? What you think?"

He never took the time to help me read.

I stormed out the room.

CHAPTER TWENTY-THREE

CLAYTON

"I Want To Hear The Words"

Clayton flopped on his bed and grabbed the remote to turn the TV on. When nothing interested him he flung it across the room just as Fashna was walking by on the way to her room.

Moving slowly.

"Fash, come here for a sec."

He sat on the edge of the bed and watched her shuffle inside, holding her stomach. He was getting irritated that Kennard only saw Tristan.

What about him?

He could move in the streets just like his gay brother if given a chance. He was growing weary and the only thing that soothed him was being in charge of the girls.

Especially Fashna.

"Yes, Clayton?" She entered the doorway but hung there.

"Come in and sit down."

She walked slowly into the room and sat next to him on the bed, before playing with her fingernails. Her timid manner made him feel more empowered, which was why he chose her as his main conquest. The others oozed strength from their native country and weren't so easily manipulated. With the exception of Tano he felt they would be more trouble than they were worth.

But Fashna was very submissive.

Just like he preferred them.

"How you feeling?"

She understood him. "Better…still weak."

He nodded and ran his thumb down her face. "Do you like when I make love to you?" He gripped his crotch. "When I serve up this good dick?"

She nodded but her stiffness told him she felt otherwise. "Yes, sir."

"What I tell you about calling me sir up here?" He frowned. "I only need you to do that around the others so that they know I'm in charge. And not showing favoritism and shit. It's a professional thing." He gripped the back of her neck. "If you weren't different I wouldn't have told my mother to keep you up here until you were completely good."

"Thank you, sir...I mean Clayton." With wide eyes she looked at him, wondering if she'd angered him again and would she be punished.

"Why do you like what I do to you? I want to hear the words."

She swallowed the lump in her throat. "But my English is not good."

"I know you understand me, Fashna. Use the best English possible."

"It hurts...sometimes," she whispered. "When you are on me."

His lips tightened because he didn't care about her feelings. Kennard hurt him by not wanting him on the block and he wanted his ego stroked and he wanted her to do it. "I thought you liked it." He crossed his arms over his chest.

"I do...but sometimes...not so much."

He frowned. "So you like laying on the floor with a bunch of bitches in the basement?" He paused. "Instead of being up here with me?"

"No...I like it, Clayton. But...I'm not well—"

"If you don't want to be up here then go back. I'll let my mother know living up here with the rich folk is too much for you." He walked across his room and grabbed a pack of cigarettes to support a habit he just picked up. "Matter of fact, get out."

She walked toward him. "Please, Clayton...I...I want you. I just...don't...I'm sorry." She grabbed his hand. "I'm just afraid of...your mother."

"Why you afraid of her?"

"She treats us...mean." She gripped his hand tighter. "And I'm scared." She paused. "I know you...I know you can't help. And she's in charge but—"

He pulled away from her. "Nobody is in charge of me." He frowned pointing in her face.

"Then you can help me?"

Clayton searched his mind for an answer he could give her that wouldn't make it seem like he had zero power. When he couldn't find one he said, "Nobody is going to scare you anymore." He raised his chin.

"But how?"

"Because I'm gonna get you pregnant and then you gonna have my baby." He smiled just thinking about it. "You gonna be served this good dick every night until you carrying my seed."

CHAPTER TWENTY-FOUR

ZOE

"The Purpose Is Money"

These girls are going to make me snap on them. We're opening in five minutes and the prep work necessary to run smoothly isn't done.

What's wrong with them?

I walked past Sam, the new security guard Valla hired and introduced me to since Clayton wasn't reliable enough to make sure the girls don't escape. He was always watching and I liked that about him because he didn't miss a thing.

He even watched me.

A little too closely at times.

I stood in the middle of the floor and clapped my hands. "I don't know what you bitches doing but you better put some pep in your step." I looked at the digital watch on my arm. "Customers will be here in five minutes and I expect everybody to be ready to receive them. No running around looking for hair and capes. Everything needs to be at your stations."

The girls moved slowly and I felt something was off. “Tano, come back with me to my office.”

She placed her broom against the wall and followed. Once there I handed her a McDonald’s bag filled with food I didn’t want. I sat behind my desk, she on the other side. “I like you, Tano. A lot.”

“I like you too, ma’am,” She responded with a thick accent as she bit down into the McMuffin. “Thank you for the food.”

“I may have a job for you.” I paused. “I need you to look over your friends and make sure they do the right thing. That they aren’t plotting on me. Can I count on you?”

“Of course, ma’am.” Her mouth was full.

I stood up and sat on the edge of the desk. “Is there anything that I need to know about the girls? Anything at all?”

She swallowed and put her food down. “Serwa doesn’t like you ma’am.”

From where I sat I looked out onto the floor and saw her talking to Lumo who made it clear she hated me many times. “Is that so?”

“Yes and—”

"What are you doing in my office?" Valla asked breathing heavily walking inside, interrupting our conversation. She flung her purse on the desk. "And why isn't Tano on the floor?" She placed her hands on her hips.

"Tano, sit over there." I pointed to a chair in the corner and she grabbed her food and moved quickly out the way. "I'm talking to her, Valla. Why else would she be here?"

"That still doesn't explain why you in my office."

"We handle business here. What's the problem?"

"The problem is that this is my personal space. And I don't want you here, especially not workers." She paused. "Do you get it now?"

I laughed. "We're running this shop and we can't always take care of things out on the floor. So unless you gonna knock down another wall and make some more room, this is it."

"Well speaking of running the shop come out here with me for a second. I have to meet with the girls and you need to hear this too." She walked out and I followed. When we made it to the floor the girls were at their stations waiting on clients.

"Listen up, I'm increasing quota by $50.00 per girl," Valla advised them. "I don't care how you do it just get it done." She paused. "Do all of you understand?" She looked at the women who remained silent. Like she wasn't speaking to them. When they didn't respond she grew uneasy. "Open your fucking mouths."

I looked at the women and nodded that it was okay to speak.

"Yes, ma'am, we understand," Serwa finally said.

Valla's eyes widened with anger. "So you don't address me until she says so?" She yelled. "I don't know what the fuck is going on here but this is my shop!" She pointed at the floor. "And when I ask a question you answer directly to me."

I laughed and shook my head because this spectacle was ridiculous and a complete waste of time. At the end of the day things were running smoothly and we didn't need her around these parts. "Valla, just go home." I looked toward her office. "Tano. Bring Valla's purse out here."

When Valla turned her head Tano was holding her bag and the security guard was standing next to me. Valla looked at him and then Tano before snatching her purse.

"I know you want to be helpful, Valla, but we don't need you," I said calmly. "So please, don't come back without calling first."

"*Without calling*? I don't have to call before I come." She pointed at the floor. "This is my establishment."

"I know it is, Valla. We all do. Honestly." I said sarcastically. "But the purpose is money. And right now you're fucking with the flow. So please leave."

She looked at the girls and me again. "Kennard is going to hear about this shit, you sloped faced bitch." She stormed out.

Sam stepped up to me, too close, like he always did. "You need anything else, ma'am?" He paused. "Want me to tell you if she comes back before I let her in?"

"Yeah," I looked at Valla stomping to her car. "That would be nice."

"No problem," he touched me on the shoulder and walked off and I moved toward the office with Tano on my heels.

I heard the doorbell chime and knew customers were entering. From my view I saw Fashna who had been dropped off for the first time since she was sick. The girls rushed her with hugs because they hadn't seen her in weeks.

"Everybody get back to work!" I yelled. "The reunion is over!"

When the girls scrambled I saw Fashna glare at me and place a red cape around a customer's neck.

"Ma'am, did you hear about friend?" Tano said. "I mean...Fashna's new friend?"

I frowned. "What you talking about?"

"The client she has today...canceled many appointments until she could get Fashna. She only likes Fashna to do hair. And brother comes every time. He's from Kenya and speaks our language."

My heart rate increased "What are you saying?"

"He like's Fashna, ma'am. Might be problems for you later."

I stood up and walked to the doorway, glancing on the floor. Fashna was braiding her client and across the room was a very handsome stranger who was staring intently in her direction.

This nigga gotta go.

CHAPTER TWENTY-FIVE

SERWA

"We're Stronger Than Them"

"We don't have to wait anymore now that Fashna is back," Serwa whispered before hugging her again. They (Serwa, Fashna, Lumo, Tano and Kessie) were talking quietly in the basement once more about an escape plan. With Fashna's return there was no longer a reason to wait. "I say we move tonight."

"Friends, please don't do this," Fashna pleaded. "We tried before and you remember what happened. What if we make a mistake again and someone else is killed? My heart couldn't suffer such a loss."

Serwa stared at Fashna as if she didn't recognize her. "So you are trusting them now?" She frowned. "After everything they've done to us? Just because you lie in Clayton's bed nightly?"

"It's not that," Fashna said looking down at her fingers. "It's just that...I'm afraid if we fail again one of us will get hurt."

"And you think that is a good enough reason to delay?" Lumo questioned, her nostrils flaring. "Because the only reason we didn't move before was because we wanted to see that you were safe. We didn't want to leave you behind, Fashna. Now you're either with us or not. Your call! Let me hear it!"

Fashna walked away. "I'm very appreciative. It's just that I don't think this is right." She sat on the floor Indian style. "I still have nightmares about Emma's face...and the blood...and the..." She looked up at them. "Can you honestly say that won't happen again? What if we kill her and nobody knows we're down here? What if we starve to death?"

Serwa and the others walked over to her and perched on the floor in front of her. "Fashna, we have to leave this place," Serwa said passionately. "The way they are treating us is not right. Don't you see that? We're stronger than these Americans. Always have been."

"I'm ready to leave too, Fashna," Kessie whispered. She was normally quiet but was growing stronger since she'd been through so much. "If I stay here one more year I'd probably kill myself." She wiped away a flowing tear. "I can't take anymore. I just can't."

Serwa gripped Kessie's hands and looked deeply into her eyes. "And I won't allow that to happen. Not while I have breath in my body." She placed a hand over her pounding heart before focusing on Fashna. "Now is the time, friend. No more delay. We must move now."

Fashna looked up at Serwa and the others. "Is everyone okay with the plan?" Serwa, Lumo, Tano and Kessie all said yes. "Then I guess I'm ready too. Besides, my body can't handle anymore of Clayton's sexual abuse. And he's trying to impregnate me. I'd die if I have a child of a monster."

Serwa hugged her tightly, the musk from her underarms was overpowering. The girls were only allowed a shower once a week, having to settle for sink wash ups during the other days. So they all were strong, often offending their customers.

"I'm glad, friend," Serwa said passionately. "So when she comes down with the food I will yank her ugly ass to the floor. Once she's down Lumo you run up the steps with the keys to open the door."

"I got it," Lumo winked. "Let's do this shit."

"And with Lumo overhearing Clayton telling Sam that he's going to the basketball game tonight we must act fast." Serwa looked at her friends. "Ready or not we're moving tonight."

An hour later Zoe came down with sandwiches to feed them. The women faked sleep on their cots but the moment Zoe's foot touched the last step Tano jumped in front of her to protect her. "Ma'am, don't come down here! Serwa is going to hurt you!"

Serwa leaped to her feet in anger. "You rotten, bitch!" she yelled in African. "A fucking snake you are!"

Afraid of being attacked Zoe ran back and she allowed Tano to follow. Once upstairs, in the kitchen, Tano told her all about the plan and for her snake-ish behavior Zoe awarded her new privileges. But as they sat at the kitchen table there was still one question above all others she wanted to know.

Zoe gripped Tano's hands. "Tano, what *really* happened to Emma? I must know." Her eyes widened and her body trembled. If Tano went this far as to save her maybe she would finally learn the truth. “Was it really an accident?”

Tano searched her mind for the right words to say. She knew if she implemented the girls she would be implementing herself too. Slowly her eyes met Zoe’s. “It was an accident, ma’am.” She swallowed. “Really.”

Not liking what she learned, Zoe released her grip and stared at her intently. “For your sake I better never find out that you’re lying. You bush bitch!”

Clayton clutched a knife in his palm as he, Zoe and Tano stomped downstairs later that night. Aiming the blade at the women he instructed each one to return to the cage.

Except Serwa.

After Clayton tied Serwa’s arms behind her back and her ankles together, Zoe sat down in front of where she was perched on the floor.

"You dirty, bitch, " Serwa said in perfect English before shooting a glob of spit mixed with blood in her face. It hung on her eyelash and slid onto her nose.

Disgusted, Zoe slid it off and slapped her hard. "You're going to wish you hadn't done that shit." She stood up and looked back at Clayton. "Take out everything you hate about life on this bitch and leave her limp."

Clayton handed Zoe the knife and rubbed his hands together briskly. He was preparing to have a good violent time. When he was done he kicked Serwa in her face, chest, back and body repeatedly. His blows were so strong that her body went limp as blood and food spewed from her lips.

"I'm going to kill you," Lumo cried from the bars, as the others remained silent, too afraid to speak up for fear they'd be next. Seeing her friend treated so roughly enraged her and Lumo didn't give a fuck. "Do you hear me, Zoe? I'm going to kill you ugly bitch."

Zoe laughed. "Just try it."

When Clayton was tired Zoe bent down and got in Serwa's face again. "I know you don't understand why I have to beat you. You aren't smart enough to comprehend so I'm not surprised," she said quoting what Mrs. Xavier said to her a long time ago. She didn't even realize she was doing it. "But if I don't punish you, you'll think it's okay for you to rebel against someone who is taking care of you. I rule your life, Serwa. Me. The moment you start understanding this I'll show you mercy but not until then."

"I hate you."

"You got three hours to rest. Afterwards, I expect you to be ready for work. No more days off for you whores. I don't care if you're oozing blood from your eyes." Zoe raised her leg and stomped her face.

CHAPTER TWENTY-SIX

ZOE

"I Did What Was Necessary"

Kennard and I have been having problems and although he didn't say it I had a feeling it was because of Valla and the argument we had in the shop the other day.

After seeing Serwa's bruised face and being questioned by customers she decided that I wasn't running the shop properly. Despite all of the girls pulling well over the extra money she requested since my beat down of Serwa.

I figured it was best to talk to her privately before things went any further and she ruined my relationship.

I walked into Valla's house in a suburb of Maryland and sat down at the dining room table. Without saying anything to me she poured us both glasses of wine. As she got situated I took a look around her home, surprised at how comfortable everything was. The color scheme was bright and it put me at ease. Maybe she's not as bad as I thought.

"I'm glad you called, Zoe." She said crossing her ankles. "Because I'm going to tell my brother that the arrangement we have at my shop ain't working for me."

My temples immediately throbbed. "So you told me it was cool to come over just so you can fire me in person?"

"That's one of the reasons." She smiled. "Truthfully I prefer to have all of my important discussions face to face." She took another sip of wine. "You can understand that can't you?" She placed it down. "Even if you don't I don't give a fuck."

"Is this because of Serwa? Because I did what was necessary to get the money you wanted. I know she looked a little banged up but it was business."

"She could barely walk, Zoe." She frowned. "The only reason you keep fucking with that girl is because you think she had something to do with killing Emma." She shook her head. "It's my fault though. I should have taken them out of your house when Kennard asked me to long ago."

She paused. "Which brings me to the second reason for inviting you over."

My eyes widened. "What else?"

"Kennard has been known to make some crass decisions in his lifetime. Some of them were necessary because of the characters he invited into his life. But every one of his decisions I helped him clear up. And this relationship with you will be another one."

I shot up. "What are you talking about, Valla?" I glared down at her.

"Sit down, Zoe." Her voice was calm, unlike the anxiety I felt at the moment.

"What do you mean my relationship is another one?" I persisted.

"Have some fucking respect in my house and sit the fuck down!" She yelled.

Slowly I took a seat. "Valla, I know we had a disagreement when I told you to call first. And I know you were even angrier about Serwa's face, but you don't know the work that goes into earning enough profit from them girls. And having to manage them! I'm doing what's necessary to keep the business going."

"So you're saying the extra money I give you as a stipend to keep the girls in your house is not enough? Because them girls are skin and bones so you can't be spending real money on food. We're talking thousands of dollars here, Zoe. On top of you, Kennard and Clayton's salaries."

I sat back in my seat. "I'm not saying that."

"Then what you saying?"

"I'm saying that profits have been raised three different times. Once by us and twice by you and I have done all I can to make sure it's earned. So when you come into the shop and undermine my authority it looks bad."

"Nobody is undermining your authority." She pointed at me. "That's my shop and I know you don't understand that since you were born a slave."

Silence.

She poured herself another glass of wine as my jaw twitched. "I blessed you and Kennard when you had nothing. The streets was saying that he was dead if he stepped back in the dope game and I wanted to protect him. That's why I pulled you both in. Yeah he's making a little money now but before my help ya'll would've starved."

"So what does this have to do with my relationship?"

"I'll tell you what it has to do with you. I'm gonna let my brother know he doesn't need you in his house. And that I want you and your son out of my shop and back on the streets where you belong." She pointed at the window and winked. "You should have never crossed me."

She's cold.

My heart pounded so hard I placed my hand over it for fear it would pop out of my chest. "What would make you think he would do that? He loves me."

"I know although I can't understand why," she smirked. "That's why I'm going to lie to him."

My eyes widened.

"Lie about what?"

"I'm gonna tell him that you fucking the security guard I hired. That I led your way." She laughed. "Have you noticed how he talks closely to you? But what you didn't notice was that whenever he does I'm somewhere near snapping pics." She laughed. "Half of your face is slacked, you walk funny and you don't have your looks anymore, Zoe. He's looking for a reason to dump you. How about I'm 'bout to give it to him."

I felt queasy. "He won't believe you."

She laughed harder. "Just like he didn't believe me when I lied on Gina?" She paused. "When I said she fucked the hit boy?" She laughed. "Yes, Zoe, he will definitely believe me. He always does."

My temples throbbed and my heart rate increased. I don't know what kind of relationship he had with his sister but I do know he broke up with Gina behind her. And if he does it to me too where will my boys and me go? We can't return to the street.

WE CAN'T!

"Valla, please don't do this. I don't want to...I don't want to hurt you. Please don't turn me into that person."

Valla's eyes widened and she leaned toward Zoe. "Hold up. Did you just say 'hurt me'?" She pointed to herself. "Do you have any idea the number of people I killed? The number of lives ruined behind my bullets?"

"I have no idea, Valla." Tears streamed down my cheeks. "But knowing how far you will go makes me realize I don't have a choice. I will kill you if I must." I blinked a few times.

She laughed. "Do you know what it takes to kill someone? Do you know the emotions required to push past fear?"

I shook my head. "I've never killed a thing in my life, even though I wanted too many times."

"Then how do you think you'll be able to kill me?"

She crossed her arms over her breasts and leaned back in the chair. I could tell I was amusing her and I understood why. A little over a year ago I was a slave. I was forced to live life for my owners and my soul was not my own. Every day I woke up I would be told what to do, what to eat and when to sleep. But having that kind of life didn't make me weak it made me more deadly.

Because I know what it's like to be free and I was not willing to give it away.

For anyone.

"I haven't thought that far, Valla. And to be honest I don't want this for us, or our family, so I'm asking that you don't lie to Kennard."

She leaned back and looked at me slowly from my feet to my eyes. “You said you would kill me so do it.” She paused. “The knives are in the kitchen. Choose any one and do your thing.” She rose from the table and sat on the sofa under the window in the living room. Then she crossed her ankles and turned on the TV.

“Valla, are you still saying you gonna lie on me? Are you gonna tell Kennard something I didn’t do?”

She laughed again. “The knives are in the kitchen...pick your favorite, Zoe. And make it quick. I don’t feel like sitting around all day waiting to die.”

I got up and crept into the kitchen while looking at her every so often. She didn’t seem bothered and the anger swelling inside me was great.

She took me as a joke.

Maybe I was.

I saw the wooden knife rack next to the fridge and grabbed the biggest knife I could find. The cool handle was in my hand and I eased over to her. She hadn’t bothered to look up from the television.

"Picked the one you liked yet?" she asked.

"Yeah..."

"So what you waiting on?" She pressed buttons on the remote. "Do it, Zoe." I walked closer and felt my body tremble. Suddenly she seemed frustrated and grabbed my wrist and placed the blade next to her throat. "Let me help you." Her eyes peered into mine. "Plunge deeply and stop fucking around. I'm ready for this shit."

Her eyes penetrated my soul and I realized she knew me better than I knew myself.

I was afraid and she was feeding on it like blood to a mosquito.

"You don't have it in you." She snatched the knife and tossed it on the sofa. "You disgust me. Get out my house and be ready to find somewhere else to stay. Because when I'm done with Kennard he won't have shit else to do with you."

Humiliated, I walked over to the table and snatched my purse. My feet seemed heavy as I moved toward the door. Life seemed to flash before my eyes because I didn't want to leave Kennard or my home. He taught me, Clayton and Tristan how to drive and provided us with documents for our identification. Because of him we were citizens. He was my world. He was teaching Tristan how to read and even started helping me.

Who was I without him?

I was out of her house and inside my truck when suddenly I realized I couldn't go. I had to do what was necessary.

But what?

I clutched the steering wheel, took a deep breath and pressed on the gas pedal. Within seconds my truck was barreling over her lawn and before I could change my mind, the front of the vehicle rolled over the couch in the living room. I didn't need to guess if I struck her because when I looked down the top part of her body was under my right wheel.

Her intestines hung out of her mouth and the pupil of her right eye was too far to the left.

But was she still alive?

Taking a deep breath I backed up and pushed through the house again. I'd gone so far I couldn't turn around. If this was going to be worth it I needed to make sure she was dead and think about the consequences later.

So that's what I did.

It's funny.

Her fat ass wasn't laughing now.

CHAPTER TWENTY-SEVEN

WOODY

"I'll Kill You Myself"

Woody pulled out his key and walked through Kennard's house holding the money from the recent work in a rugged blue duffle. These days Kennard didn't trust a lot of folks but with Woody and Tristan at his side he could rest easy. These youngins have already given him their souls.

As instructed, Woody bent the corner to head to a locked closet on the first floor. He was about to unlock the door and place the money inside when he saw Fashna standing before him. She was prettier than he remembered.

Her light skin was flushed with red splotches due to being nervous and her hair was in a tight bun on top of her head as usual. He was immediately attracted to her but knew it could never be. She was a slave and he was an upcoming drug lord.

There was something going on in the house that he wasn't aware of so he had to keep his distance.

The less he knew about the better.

After Emma, who he fell for before she died, he made a decision not to deal with women. It was all about stacking his paper and buying a new house in Virginia for the bachelor's life. Besides, they were too much trouble and he needed a clear mind. He held to his vow and kept bitches at arms length until he saw Fashna about to be stabbed by Zoe.

He thought about her ever since.

"Hi," she smiled and waved. "It's Woody right?"

Woody raised his chin as his answer and unconsciously touched his freshly braided hair. "Yeah...that's me."

Fashna moved closer. "Ms. Zoe and Kennard are gone," she said with a heavy African accent, her English getting better by the day.

"Yeah...I know." He pulled the bag closer to him. Since he wasn't sure what her play was in the household he didn't want her to see the money spot in the closet.

"Can I get you something to drink?" She questioned.

He cleared his throat. "Yeah, some water would be cool."

He was actually parched but could use the diversion to tuck the money away without her knowing. And the moment she disappeared into the kitchen that's exactly what he did. When the money was hidden he locked the door right before she came back with the water.

Woody gulped the beverage down and wiped his mouth with the back of his hand. "Thanks." He handed her the cup. "But I gotta go." He pointed at the door with his thumb.

He was about to spin around until she grabbed his wrist. "Help me...please." She was no longer cordial and looked like she saw a ghost.

He stared down at her hand and pushed it off. "Help you do what?"

Tears streamed down her face. "They're going to kill me," she whispered. "Please. Take me anywhere. Just away from here."

Woody was confused because he asked himself one question since the first day he saw Fashna about to be stabbed by Zoe. And it was...would he have helped if he could do it over again?

His response was always the same.

Yes.

So what was the difference now?

"You got some place to go?" He asked.

"I'll go anywhere," she said excitedly, hands clutched in front of her. "I don't care where it is."

He scratched his sore scalp and looked up before looking down. This was a matter he had to give serious thought to. When his decision was made he took a deep breath. "Well come on."

He rushed toward the front door and she was on his heels. Inside the car she was so excited to be escaping she could barely contain herself. Clayton's nightly rapes were tearing at her insides, making her ache daily. She needed to be away from Zoe and her crazy son.

Forever.

Once inside Woody's car she was relieved.

But Woody pulled out of the driveway and was heading down the street when his temples throbbed.

He gripped at the steering wheel, already feeling the pressures of his disloyalty. He was honorable which was why he was constantly torn. "I can't do this," he said to himself.

Fashna positioned her body and looked at him, sensing her worse fears becoming reality. The day someone would agree to help and then change their mind.

It couldn't end like this.

It just couldn't.

After she heard about how Clayton beat Serwa she realized if she didn't want to deal with the rapes she would have to be subjected to the beating. She was willing to go anywhere but back to that house.

"Please don't." She covered her quivering lips with her fingertips. "I can't go back. He rapes me and—"

He looked at her and pointed in her face. "This ain't my fuckin' fight!" He focused back on the road.

"I'm begging you." She cried shaking her head rapidly. "I'm afraid."

"LIKE I SAID, THIS AIN'T MY FUCKING FIGHT!" He yelled in her face. "Kennard does good by me and doing this shit right here is a slap in his face!" He pointed downward. "And I'm not with it!"

Fashna moved uneasily in her seat. If he wasn't going to help her she would have to help herself. When he came to a stop sign she opened the door and was about to jump out when he gripped her hair and shirt and took off down the road.

The flapping open door didn't stop his stride all the way back to Kennard's driveway.

Once there he picked her up, kicking and screaming and stuffed her back into the house. Once in the living room he tossed her on the floor and pointed down at her. "If I find out you told them I took you out this crib you won't have to worry about Zoe because I'll kill you myself."

"You're weak!" Fashna screamed. "You're not a man like the men in Africa." She beat her chest once. "You're fucking weak." Her English came out crystal because she was angry.

Woody's nostrils flared. "Well get one of them to save you then, bitch!" He slammed the door and locked it.

He told himself he was done but the guilt of leaving her behind weighed on his conscious and he was battling with what was right.

CHAPTER TWENTY-EIGHT

KENNARD & TRISTAN

ONE MONTH LATER

"Keep Your Hearts Clean And Stay Focused"

"Why you keep coming at me about that chick?" Tristan asked Woody as they waited for Kennard to come out the trap house and go to the next spot.

Tristan was in the front seat and Woody was in back.

"Because it got my head fucked up that's why," he whispered through clenched teeth. "You know your brother in their raping shawty right? What the fuck ya'll got going on in that spot?"

Tristan frowned when he heard what his brother was doing. What his family didn't know was that even though Emma's rape fucked with Zoe's head, it messed with Tristan's even more. He felt like shit not being able to help his sister when Mrs. Xavier had those men rape her.

"My brother wouldn't do no shit like that."

"The nigga is mold, Tristan. The black shit you find hanging around the toilet. You and me both know he be raping bitches." He paused. "Now I got love for Kennard. The nigga had me since I was a pup but I'm not with this new shit he on."

"So what you saying?"

"I'm saying either check up on that shit or I will."

Kennard walked up to Bambi Kennedy (The Plug) and her partners, Race, Denim and Scarlett. They were four of the most beautiful women he'd ever seen in his lifetime, three black and one white with fire red hair.

Tristan stood next to him while Woody hung outside the spot. Behind the women were five men who were armed and aimed in their direction. Although the scene was intense it was purely for precaution. Bambi was D.C.'s biggest drug connect but the beef she earned with Abd

Al-Qadir of Saudi Arabia made her a hot target. The billionaire was coming for her pretty head.

"Thanks for meeting with me, Bambi," Kennard said as he shook her hand and placed a black duffle bag stuffed with bills on the table between them. "I know it's short notice."

"It's not a problem." She reached into the pocket of the green army fatigue cargo's she was wearing and pulled out a stick of gum before folding it into her mouth. "You come highly respected. Or else you wouldn't be looking at my face."

He nodded. "Thank you." When he found himself looking at her a little too long he changed his vision. Bambi being powerful made her sexy but her beauty sealed the deal.

The long black weave she wore was dressed in cascading curls that hung down the back of her wife beater. She was a mixture of power and femininity and he admired Kevin for bagging her.

Bambi handed the bag to Race Kennedy, who opened it and inspected its contents. Like the others she was beautiful and married to a Kennedy. At the end of the day they all were taken. "It's all here." She zipped it up.

Bambi nodded and one of the men across the room disappeared into a door and returned with another duffle. He placed it on the table and Kennard scanned its contents before handing it to Tristan. "I'm sure I'll be in contact soon."

Everyone in the room caught the chemistry between them but their professionalism wouldn't allow for much more. Besides, Kennard had a woman at home whose desire for attention took all of his time. And left him feeling drained.

After shaking hands Kennard eased in the passenger seat, Tristan in the back while Woody piloted the car. Once inside his cell phone beeped and he saw a message from Clayton.

So you neva gonna let me help?

Kennard placed the phone in his pocket. "Listen, if something were to ever happen to me I don't want Clayton around my shit. I don't trust him, Tristan." He paused and looked at Woody too. "He has the same way about him that Morgan did which means trouble."

Woody shook his head because this confirmed what Fashna was saying that something was off.

Way off.

"I got it, sir," Tristan said.

Kennard looked at both of them. "Both of ya'll are good little niggas. You keep your hearts clean and stay focused. Look out for each other because it's hard to find real niggas nowadays."

Tristan smiled and Woody continued to guide the car.

Once Woody was outside of his house he gave Kennard and Tristan dap and walked inside. Still mad about Fashna.

Kennard eased in the driver seat and was about to pull off when the radio station played Marvin Gaye, Valla's favorite singer.

When his sister died because someone slammed into the house and killed her it fucked up his head. He went into goon mode by flipping his money to supply his soldiers. Things were heavier when Zoe's truck was stolen the same day. He was so involved that he never took the time to grieve. Valla had shit with her but they were family, the only blood relative he knew and he missed her dearly. "Sir...you okay?" Tristan asked from the passenger seat.

Kennard exhaled. "Yeah, son. I'm fine." He looked ahead.

Tristan and Gasper, one of Kennard's most loyal soldiers were cooking crack in the kitchen of one of Kennard's trap houses. Originally Kennard was going to come but after being out of it over Valla, Tristan dropped him off, leaving him to catch Gasper alone.

Besides, Kennard didn't need to go for the cook. His young pups had it covered.

When they were done chefing and packaging they both plopped down at the table. "Man, after that shit I need a beer and some pussy," Gasper said pointing at the bricks. He was a tall slender kid, of 20 years with fine hair that he kept cut into a wild Mohawk. "What you trying to do? Check after these bitches with me?"

Tristan laughed. "Naw, man, I see the chicks you roll with. Ain't my speed."

Gasper sat back in his seat and tilted his head. "Fuck you trying to say? I only deal with birds?"

"I ain't trying to say nothing. Your bitches be on some other shit out here." Tristan stood up. "Burning niggas dicks and shit." He shook his head. "Naw, fam, I'll pass." He paused. "But let me run to the bathroom right quick and then we'll lock up." Tristan was pissing when suddenly the door opened. "I'm in here, man!" He yelled.

"I know," Gasper said looking at his dick and then his eyes. "Tell me to get out and I will."

Tristan's body immediately heated up. What was happening? He didn't know that gay men could pick each other out instantly but he was about to find out.

Gasper walked up to him and dropped to his knees. "Let me work you off."

"Get back, man," Tristan said angrily with his arm extended. "I'm not fucking around with you! Move back!"

"I got you, Tristan," he persisted. "Trust me. We good."

His mind said no but his penis was stiff and before he knew it Gasper was sucking his dick like a peppermint stick. Gasper was a pro so it took him all of one minute to bring Tristan to a full orgasm.

When done he swallowed his cum, stood up and wiped his mouth. “You see. All done.”

Tristan was frozen as he tried to understand what happened. What was all of that shit Gasper was just talking in the living room? About the girls? Wasn’t he straight? He had no clue that the women Gasper traveled with were beards and that his true passion was dick. Nothing about Gasper spelled gay, including his masculinity and Tristan was overwhelmed.

“Don’t worry about it, Tristan. I won’t say shit if you don’t.” He walked to the door. “Oh and since I hooked you up, you clean up and lock up the trap.” He winked. “I’m out.”

Tristan scrubbed the trap from top to bottom. He cleaned it so well that the spot look new. It wasn’t a requirement but he felt ashamed to go home right away. Ashamed to face his mother and Kennard after what he’d done.

Why did he have this desire when he wanted no parts of it?

Afterwards he placed his curly fro, which had come unraveled in a bun that sat on the top of his head. When the water he had been boiling finally reached the right temperature he walked over to it. He took several deep breaths, clenched his fist and dunked it into the scolding hot water.

"AHHHHHHHHH!" he screamed.

CHAPTER TWENTY-NINE

ZOE

"I Treat These Girls With Respect"

After I killed Valla, and convinced Kennard that my truck was stolen to hide the damage, I wasn't home a lot. My focus was keeping the shop running and profit was so good now money was overflowing. I had more than I could spend. But my absence also left room for Fashna's snake ass to take over my house and I needed that to stop. She cooked dinner, breakfast and lunch like this was her crib.

Who did she think she was?

She was a slave who needed to be reminded about her place. But when I told Kennard I wanted her gone he gave me the blues. Saying that Clayton and Tristan needed the meals and the clean house since I was unavailable.

It's like he takes everyone's side but mine.

I just entered the house and I could smell a meal that was recently cooked. Fashna was in the kitchen drying her hands on a white towel looking my way. She must've just finished washing dishes.

"Hello, Ms. Zoe." She placed the towel on the refrigerator's door handle. "Can I get you anything?" I see she was speaking better English, which irritated me too.

I tossed my purse on the couch. "Where is Kennard?"

"Him and Tristan just left."

I rolled my eyes. "Go bring my other cell phone." I took off my high heel shoes. "It's in my room charging by the bed upstairs."

"Yes ma'am." She quickly walked away.

When she returned she handed me my iPhone. "Why you didn't bring the cord?" I frowned. "What I'm gonna do with this?"

Her eyebrows rose. "Oh, I'm sorry. Right away, Ms. Zoe." She disappeared up the steps again.

When she returned I sent her up and down about twenty times more. As she lie on the floor exhausted I smiled. I bet she wouldn't have time to cook dinner tonight.

She looked at me and I could see a hint of anger. "Ms. Zoe, can I ask question?"

"What?"

"Do you not like me?"

I grinned. "What's obvious needs no confirmation."

I didn't know how to read well yet but there were two things I did learn. One was how to count money and the other was shopping. I was walking through Mazza Gallerie with two bodyguards after shutting the shops down. They were holding my shopping bags and we were on our way out when I spotted Mr. and Mrs. Xavier. Immediately a sense of fear overcame me and I started to run. Until I remembered I was no longer a slave and they couldn't hurt me.

"Zoe?" Mrs. Xavier said as she eyed me up and down before looking at my guards. "Is that you?"

I was wearing a tight royal blue dress that hugged my curves and a pair of black Christian Louboutins like the ones I use to covet in her closet. Removing my brown Louis Vuitton shades

I smiled. I could only imagine the thoughts running through their minds.

"Yes, it is." I said calmly. "And how are you? Still selling bodies?"

"But...how...I mean..." her words trailed off while Mr. Xavier continued to eyeball me. Now his gazed rolled from my feet to my breasts.

"Zoe, what happened to your face?" he asked. "You look...different."

I touched my cheek. I forgot about my stroke and suddenly I felt unworthy. Until I remembered I still had a body and ugly or not, I was rich.

"Don't worry about all of that." I paused. "Just know that what took you ten years to build took me two." I looked at both of them. "I guess I wasn't a dumb slave after all."

Mr. Xavier moved the knot on his tie from left to right, which seemed to press against his throat. "I'm happy for you, Zoe." He told me while looking deeply into my eyes. "Very happy." He continued. "How are the kids?"

I ignored him because I didn't want to talk about losing Emma. Besides, my real problem was with his wife. At least with Mr. Xavier it was fair exchange no robbery. I had sex with him, willingly sometimes to keep my family together. In my opinion we had an understanding but she was another subject.

As I looked at her I recalled her throwing me and my kids out on the street with nowhere to go that day. She would never understand the fear I had as a mother of not being able to protect my family...in an unfamiliar world.

I walked up to her and when I was close enough I slapped her. Mr. Xavier attempted to move toward me but my bodyguards dropped my bags and aimed barrels at their heads.

"Don't be stupid, Mr. Xavier," I suggested. "These men aren't trained to give warnings. They're trained to kill."

"You black, bitch!" Mrs. Xavier yelled holding her thin bloody lips.

"Yes, and I'm the black bitch who just slapped you too." I put my shades on. "Have a nice day." I shrugged. "Or not." I walked away, with my men following.

Fashna was massaging my feet so well I felt an orgasm was brewing. I was about to dose off when Kennard walked inside our room. His eyes widened and he placed a bag on the bed and stared at me. "Fashna, you can go prepare dinner."

"But, baby..." I said.

"Go," he said louder pointing at her.

When she shuffled out he sat next to me. "What are you doing?" He frowned. "Why you posted up like this?"

"I was getting my feet massaged until you came home. What's wrong? Why you in a bad mood?"

He exhaled. "I have a lot going on right now, Zoe. But nothing is more important to me than you and this family." He placed his warm hand on my thigh. "With my sister dead I need to make sure we get things back on track in my crib. And you're taking this slave shit a little too seriously for my taste." He sighed. "I would think you would be the last person participating in this shit. And yet you falling right in line."

"Why would I have a problem when I'm giving them a home? If you ask me I'm saving their lives." I stood up and walked to the door to grab my silk robe. The air conditioning was on too high. "I treat these girls with respect, Kennard."

"Why is the door locked to the basement, Zoe? And where is the fucking key? I tried to get in and couldn't a minute ago."

I rolled my eyes. "I thought you said you didn't want to know about what's going on down there."

"I changed my mind."

I shook my head. "So you think it's cool to go down into the basement where a bunch of young women roam around naked?" I paused. "It would be like walking into a woman's locker room and they need their privacy. You know that."

He walked up to me and placed his hands on the side of my face. He was squeezing so hard it hurt. "I'm a thug, Zoe. I know that. I do shit that don't sit right with a lot of people. But I'm also a man in love with a woman I see changing before my eyes."

"So now this is about my looks?"

He released me. "I don't give a fuck about your looks and I'm not feeding into that bullshit no more. I'm talking about your heart."

"Kennard, your drug operation hasn't taken off the way it needs in order to care for this family. We need them girls right now."

"When my operation is profitable...and it will be profitable...you're going to release them girls. I can't have this type of shit on my conscious, Zoe. And if you want to be with me you gonna have to shift the program."

"You're being unfair!" I yelled. "That braiding salon is not just about providing for this family. It makes me feel like I'm contributing. Tristan has you, Clayton has Fashna but what about me?"

"Keep it real. What you want is power. And a woman with that kind of ambition scares me. Not because I don't want you to achieve but because you would do anything for it. And a drive that strong makes me not trust you. And if you're in my bed I need trust or you gotta get the fuck out."

CHAPTER THIRTY

ZOE

"I Need That To Change"

When I heard something fall behind me I looked back. Fashna was supposed to be carrying my bags, which included the new hair we bought for the shop and my lunch. But now my items were on the ground.

I rushed up to her. "I'm sorry, Ms. Zoe. I just –"

I slapped her. "Bitch, pick up my—"

"Excuse me, ma'am, can you tell me why you just hit that young woman?" When I turned around an elderly black woman was standing behind me.

"Do you want to tell me why you're minding my fucking business?"

The woman rolled her eyes and focused on Fashna. "Is there anything I can—"

"Hold up, don't talk to my—" I stopped myself when I was about to say 'slave'. "Listen, just leave us alone. Sca-dattle."

Instead of exiting she looked around me. "Young lady...do you need help?"

Fashna opened and closed her mouth before finally looking at me. "No...I'm fine." Her English was still limited but she was clear. Fashna picked up my bags.

The woman shrugged. "Suit yourself." She stormed off.

I rolled my eyes. When she was gone I stepped closer to Fashna. "You're one lucky bitch." I pointed in her face. "Because if that went any differently you would've paid for it dearly."

When we made it into the shop I removed my keys and unlocked the door. Nobody came in or out of the shop without the key or being allowed inside by security. I had a new bodyguard who talked less and secured the shop more and we had a good relationship.

When we were inside I said, "Put the bags in my office, Fashna."

I looked around and all the stations were neat and ready. Serwa was a troublemaker but she was also professional. She made sure that the other girls cleaned so well you could practically eat off the floor.

And *still* I didn't trust her.

I got the impression that in any minute she would attempt to get revenge. So I kept eyes on her at all times because if she tried I would be waiting.

"Okay, people, chop, chop." I clapped my hands. "We have a huge flow coming and we don't want anyone waiting longer than they have to."

When Fashna came back out I walked up to her. "Lately you been out of it and I need that to change."

"I met my quota, Ms. Zoe."

"Well start doing it with a smile." I paused. "And another thing, you're done cooking for my family unless I'm there. Am I clear?"

"Yes, Ms. Zoe." She walked away and I moved toward my office. I remembered I forgot to tell her something else when I turned around I saw her glaring at me. She didn't know I was about to turn around. If looks could kill I'd be dead.

She straightened up her face when I caught her and smiled but it was too late. I already saw her and the message was received.

Loud and clear.

CHAPTER THIRTY-ONE

FASHNA

"Don't Say Anything More"

Fashna was braiding the hair of the client whose brother liked her. She kept looking behind her because she was thinking about coming clean with the girl about her life. Realizing that if she didn't make a move soon Zoe's knife or Clayton's dick would kill her.

"You know they told me my brother couldn't come back in here right?" Diamond advised in African dialect as Fashna continued her work. "What the fuck kind of shop is this? Where a man can't accompany his sister? I've never heard of no shit like that."

Fashna looked behind her to see if the security guard was listening. Neither Zoe nor Clayton was there so she didn't have to worry that much but she had to be careful. "I can't talk to you about it, Diamond. I'm sorry."

"Why not? The only people who know the language are the braiders." She frowned. "What's going on, Fashna? Why you seem so afraid all the time?"

Her breaths were heavy because talking to her was a dangerous move. "Because I am afraid all of the time."

Diamond looked up at her. "Are they making you do this job? Like for free?"

"Yes...I...mean...no...I mean...I don't know."

"That's a damn shame. You would think after how African Americans were treated they'd show respect to their own. And love each other more." She paused. "But I'm not surprised. Westerners don't give a fuck about each other in this country. They kill each other. Take from each other and break each other down. Makes me miss the homeland you know?"

Fashna nodded and noticed the other braiders peering at them ever so often. Although Serwa and Lumo stopped coming at her about escaping, she knew an oppressed people would do anything they could to gain favor or control.

Especially Tano who despite helping Zoe that time was still placed down the basement with the rest of the girls.

"Please don't say anything more," Fashna whispered. "I've already said enough."

"Well let me say one more thing. My brother wants to meet you and if you're in trouble he can help, Fashna." Her tone was passionate. "But you must be brave enough to speak up and you must do it now."

CHAPTER THIRTY-TWO

KENNARD

"It's Different This Time"

Tristan was in the corner at the trap talking to Woody about a situation he wouldn't let rest.

"You spoke to the girl yet?" Woody whispered.

"Who?"

"Fashna."

Tristan sighed. "I'm gonna do it, but it's gonna be on my time. Pressing me out about it won't make it happen any quicker."

Woody shuffled. "You got two days and after that I'ma do whatever I feel."

"Why is this so important?" Tristan whispered. "You don't even know shawty. Why can't you just keep your mind on your paper?" He pointed at his head. "Huh?" Tristan looked behind him to see if Kennard was listening. "Are you really trying to fuck this up?"

He wasn't.

Woody backed up a little and examined Tristan as if just seeing him. "You adapting, nigga. And for the worst too."

"Why?" He frowned. "Because I won't let you pull me in on this save-a-ho shit?"

"Naw, because you don't give a fuck no more. When I met you, you wasn't like this. You weren't like your mother but now you are. What happened where ya'll came from?" He looked down. "And when did you burn your fucking hand?"

"Fuck all that," Tristan said. "I just need to know why it's any of your concern?"

"Because I saw fear in her eyes, man. The last time I saw that kind of fear I had a gun to my head and was getting robbed."

Tristan shook his head. "Look, you do what you want. Just leave me out of it."

Kennard stood in front of five of his soldiers in the trap. By his side were Tristan, Woody and

Gasper. The product he purchased from the Pretty Kings moved quickly and he was in the process of making another deal for more.

"I just need everyone to watch their surroundings. We been getting money and things have been quiet and I don't trust it. Something doesn't feel right." He paused and looked at his men. "Finish baking what's left. I'm gonna see when we can get the next—"

When there was a knock at the door Tristan reached for the hardware on his hip. The rest of the soldiers tucked the coke and when it was nowhere in sight Tristan eased slowly toward the door. Gazing out of the peephole he was irritated at what he saw.

"Who is it?" Kennard asked.

Tristan looked at him. "It's Gina," He frowned. "Want me to send her on her way?"

His eyes widened. "How the fuck this bitch know where I was?" He moved toward the door. "Naw, lil nigga. I'm gonna go talk to her right quick."

"I don't know about this, Kennard," Tristan warned. "Her showing up without an invite sounds shady to me. You sure you wanna go outside? Don't you feel like it's a set up? Let me rush her off. I can do it."

Kennard touched the top of Tristan's head and gripped the back of his neck like a father. "I want you to call me dad. You don't have my blood but you have my heart. And where I'm from that's better."

Tristan wanted nothing more than to refer to him that way. The only other person he called dad was Mr. Xavier, his real father but he never was allowed to call him that to his face. Him and Kennard's relationship was built on a foundation of mutual respect, nothing like him and Mr. Xavier. "I'd love to, dad."

Kennard took a deep breath and released him. "I know you worried about me but don't be. I'm gonna see what she want and send her on her way. You look after things here and make sure packaging runs smoothly." Kennard looked into his eyes. "I'm trusting you, son."

"And I won't let you down."

Kennard wished he'd taken Tristan's advice because Gina was yelling and screaming over still having a broken heart. Her mascara ran down her face and snot oozed from her nose, hanging onto the tip of her upper lip. She was disgusting and he wondered why he ever fucked her. When she moved out she thought he would fall and instead he prospered. This did nothing but send her through the roof.

"Gina, you left me so why you in here tripping?"

"Because you said I fucked another nigga. Your sister lied on me and you believed her."

"Don't talk about my sister." he pointed in her face. "I'm not fucking around. I will end your ass."

"I don't mean to disrespect." She wiped her tears. "But you moved another chick in like you never cared. I mean you didn't even know that ugly bitch." She sobbed as she could barely catch her breath. "We fight all the time, Kennard. We go through our problems." She wiped her eyes making her makeup smear worse. "But how many times have we broken up and gotten back together?"

"It's different this time. I don't—"

"Please don't say you don't love me. Please don't break my heart when I know it's not true. You can't tell me you don't miss me because if you didn't I wouldn't be in your truck. Let's be real with each other like we use to be."

He exhaled because she was blowing him. Everything about her turned him off in the moment and he knew he'd never get through to her. "How did you find my spot?"

"What?" she asked frowning. The last thing she wanted was to talk about his drug business. "I don't understand."

"This spot is off the grid. So how did you know where it was, Gina? I need you to be real with me."

She sighed and looked ahead as she searched her mind. "Oh...I think Morgan told me when I went to visit him. Everybody ditched him since he got life and he mad." She shrugged. "But it's been so long I can't remember." She smeared her makeup again.

Kennard scratched his head. "How the fuck he know?" He thought out loud. "That nigga locked up."

"You know it's the streets, Kennard." She grabbed a tissue from his glove compartment and wiped her face but it didn't help. "But that's not what we're discussing right now."

Kennard turned his body toward her so she could know he was serious. "It's over, Gina. And I know I played you in the past and for that I'm sorry. Had I known you would be like this when it ended I would've never gotten with you. I'm not coming back so get use to it."

"But it doesn't have to be like this." She grabbed his penis. "Just let me kiss it a little and let 'it' decide if I can come back." She moved her head toward his crotch and he pushed her off.

"You not listening, Gina. We done."

She blinked a few times and exhaled like she'd been holding her breath. He was staring in her wild eyes when suddenly he felt a blade plunging into the contents of his stomach. Had he focused on her fully he would've seen it tucked under her leg the entire time.

"Gina," he said with wide eyes as he gripped his belly. "Why?"

She looked around to see if anyone was coming and focused back on him. "I never got over you, Kennard." She rubbed her runny nose. "And I'm so sorry. I love you." She touched his face, leaving a trail of snot on his skin before dipping out.

CHAPTER THIRTY-THREE

ZOE

"You Aren't Born For This Lifestyle"

I never got use to going to the hospital and yet it was now my daily reality. Every day since they found Kennard clinging onto life in his truck I was here. Two weeks passed and he was still in a coma without any hope that he'd make it.

When I walked into his room today Tristan was there. He was sitting in the only seat but rose when he saw me. I tried to call him when I first got to the hospital but the reception here was terrible. No cell phones worked at all. "You can sit here, ma."

I sat down, scooted closer to Kennard's bed and grabbed his hand. He lost so much weight that he didn't look the same. "How is he?" I asked Tristan. "Is there any...any...change?" I felt myself about to cry and Tristan touched my shoulder.

"He's fine, ma. And I know the doctor's saying they can't help him but he's gonna pull through. I believe it in my heart." He put his hand on my chest.

I exhaled because at this point I wanted to believe anything. What bothered me is that no one knew what happened. One minute he was handling business and the next he was stabbed up in his truck. I had a feeling that Tristan knew more but he refused to say a word. His loyalty was definitely with Kennard. "Have you heard who might have done this?

He removed his hand and cleared his throat. "No. But I'm sure we'll find out soon. The only thing I want you to do is take care of yourself. I got everything else."

I looked up at him. Although he changed I didn't think he understood the level of what was happening. "Tristan, you have to be careful out there. You have to be smart because whoever did this may try to hurt you."

"They won't, ma. Trust me." His tone was confident.

I rubbed my temples. "Tristan, you weren't born for this lifestyle. Not even two years ago you were cleaning toilets. And now you a gangster? Get serious, boy."

He exhaled. “Ma, I’m with pops every day. I’m out there in the trenches.” He pointed to the window. “There’s nobody better than me to keep things running and to tell you that who did this to him, won’t be coming back for me.”

“Tristan, now that Kennard is down you’re going to stop whatever you’ve been doing immediately. The games are over and you might as well know now.”

“Sorry, I can’t do that.” He stuffed his hands in his pockets.

“That wasn’t up for discussion.”

He sighed. “I know. You’re just gonna have to trust me, ma. I know it’s hard because you look at me like a baby but I’ve seen a lot of things since I’ve been with pops.”

“First off he’s not your pops.” I frowned. “And what does that mean? You think you know him more than I do?”

“As far as business goes…yes.”

I lowered my brow. “If you disobey me you have to leave my house.”

“That seemed easy for you.” He walked away and leaned against the wall next to the bathroom. “To put me out.”

"You heard what I said."

"Fuck!" He yelled through clenched teeth. "If I was Clayton you wouldn't be treating me this fucking way. You give respect to that nigga and he didn't even earn it."

I never heard him yell at me and I was scared. "What does that mean?"

"You allow what goes on with him and the girls right under your nose."

"At least he's sleeping with women."

"I'm not what you think I am, ma."

"You can stand over there and pretend to be a thug if you want to but we both know what you really are don't we?" I rubbed my temples again to slow down the throbbing. "And we both know you want my man."

He frowned. "What? I got a girlfriend, ma. And she loves me."

I laughed. "Then why haven't you brought her home, Tristan? Why haven't I seen her?" I paused. "Listen, I want you out of my face because I've made myself clear. You stay in the streets and you don't come home. You make the choice."

CHAPTER THIRTY-FOUR

FASHNA

"Does He Ask About Me Still"

Fashna was braiding Diamond's hair, her vagina sore because Clayton raped her with a frozen water bottle earlier that morning. As the days went by he seemed to gain pleasure out of torturing her, often not using his penis but beating his dick while he put her through pain.

She was daydreaming when Diamond said, "I can't believe this shop looks like this. At one point when I came in here I wouldn't be able to find a piece of hair on the floor. What's going on? Where's the sheriff?"

"The manager has been away," Fashna said as she wiped a tear that crept up. "Her man is in a coma."

Diamond looked up at her. "That fine ass baldhead dude that be around here sometimes? I can't believe he was ever with her ass."

Fashna nodded.

"I sure feel bad for her. A woman that ugly won't ever get a man that fine again." She looked around. "She needs to hurry back because this spot is starting to look as gross as the others."

Fashna broke out sobbing and ran to the bathroom. Although the braiders were not allowed to be alone with customers Diamond followed anyway. Once inside she locked the door. "What's wrong, Fashna?"

"I...I can't talk about it."

Diamond sighed. "Why do you continue to protect these people, Fashna? Your heart is breaking and yet you still allow them to do what they will. Why? Where is the strength I can see in you?"

Fashna sat on the toilet seat. "You don't understand."

"Then explain it to me." She walked over to her. "I want to help and more than anything understand."

"Where is your brother, Diamond?" She wiped her tears away. "Does he ask about me still?"

She sighed. "I'm going to be honest, he finally got the message that you weren't interested so he hasn't mentioned a word to me. I think he may be moving in with his new girlfriend next month but I'm not certain."

Fashna gripped her hands. "Diamond, please talk to him. Please tell him I'm ready to meet."

"I'll see what I can do." She sighed. "But I can't make any promises. When do you want me to set it up?"

"Tonight. I can't delay."

Fashna sat in Maxwell's silver 7 series BMW outside of the braiding shop. The only reason she was bold was because she knew Zoe was at home grieving over Kennard's status while Clayton hadn't bothered to go to the shop at all.

After her last customer was done that night, they were told to wait for their ride. Hungry, the security guard went to the carryout when the last customer left. And since Diamond wanted to help Fashna she placed a wad of gum in the door on her way out so it wouldn't lock. This left Fashna with fifteen minutes before he returned and noticed her gone.

"I'm glad you decided to meet but I don't understand why," Maxwell whispered. "You haven't said two words to me since we met."

Fashna positioned her body to look into his eyes. "I don't trust anybody." She took a deep breath. "And it's not because I don't have a desire. It's just that...everybody around me has an agenda." She placed her hand on top of his. "And I want to trust you but I need to be sure I'm not making a mistake."

"I don't have any agendas, Fashna. So tell me what is wrong."

Fashna spent the next fifteen minutes telling him everything in their language. How she was brought to America under false pretenses. And how she was forced to braid hair and was raped repeatedly by Clayton for sport. When she was done he breathed heavily as anger coursed through his blood.

"Wow, I wasn't expecting that." He rubbed his temples and positioned himself to look into her eyes. "If you—"

Suddenly the door was yanked open from the passenger side and Fashna felt faint thinking she was caught.

Until she saw Woody's face.

Fashna was in Woody's car her arms crossed over her body. He hadn't said a word and she was certain he was taking her back to the house like he'd done before. "They'll kill me you know?" she said. Her English much better.

"I'm not taking you there." He piloted the car down the highway.

Her head spun in his direction. "Then where are we going?"

"Away from this spot." He continued to drive. "I got a hotel room for you. Had my female homie pick you up a few pieces of clothes so don't worry about your stuff."

She looked at him confusedly.

"Do you understand most of what I said?" He asked.

When a tear rolled down her face he received his answer.

"I'm sorry I didn't help you before, Fashna. But I won't make the mistake again."

Fashna sat at a chair near the window over looking Washington D.C. He wanted them as far from Baltimore as possible. The night view presented a spectacular glow of the city. She was so overwhelmed with gratitude for Woody that she cried silently as she enjoyed the view.

Needing to make a call Woody stepped away and pulled his cell phone out of his pocket. After he dialed the number he wanted, he waited for the thunder he was sure was coming. "What up, man?" Tristan said.

"I got her."

Tristan sighed. "You sure you want to do that?"

"It's already done."

Silence.

"I don't agree but I understand."

Woody was somewhat surprised. "So what this makes for our business-ship?"

"I ain't got no problem if you don't."

Woody felt relief. "Aight, well I'll get with you in a minute."

"Done."

Woody stuffed his phone back in his pocket and sat next to Fashna at the window. They enjoyed the view and it looked even better, together.

CHAPTER THIRTY-FIVE

TRISTAN

"With All Due Respect I'm Already Down The Dark Path"

"You aight, man?" Gasper asked. "Seem out of it."

Tristan cleared his throat. He had a lot on his mind. First the only man who ever treated him like a son was fighting for his life. Second, his mother didn't want any parts of him and last, his closest comrade had broken code and took Fashna.

He was also torn about not facilitating the move sooner since he disagreed with what Clayton had done to her anyway. After all he heard the many nights Fashna cried out as Clayton continuously tore at her flesh.

And on top of everything, he was still battling with his sexuality.

Was he a man or not?

"I'm cool," Tristan lied. "Just thinking about some shit."

"On another note, I know we not gonna make it through the night," Gasper said as they stood in the trap house and looked at the remaining product on the table. He sighed. "The only thing is I don't know what we gonna do with Kennard being down. We don't have the connection."

Tristan rubbed the top of his head. He knew the operation generated thousands a day and going without product crippled business tremendously. He'd been staying at a hotel in Baltimore and although he appreciated the peace he was starting to think that his mother was right. Maybe he was in over his head.

"What we gonna do, man?" Gasper asked.

Tristan sighed. "Give me an hour. I'll come up with a plan."

Tristan was digging into the soft dirt with a shovel in a patch of woodland in Maryland. Kennard took him there many times so he'd known if anything ever happened where to get the paper. Kennard didn't trust the banks and said if he was going to lose money he'd rather the earth devour it instead of a bunch of greedy white men.

Alone now, he couldn't go back to the house since he moved out after his mother demanded that he walk away from the operation. But he knew he needed more cash. Luckily Tristan was the only person Kennard trusted enough to show the earth stash.

After the money was removed he grabbed a few stacks wrapped in plastic and repacked the soil. When he was done he hustled to his car, removed his clothes and pulled some water from the trunk. It took five bottles to rinse the dirt away and get him presentable.

Now he was ready.

Bambi sat in front of Tristan with the other Pretty Kings behind her. She examined the young man's gait and more than anything his eyes. She determined that although he probably had secrets she could also trust him. "I heard about what happened to Kennard."

"I know and thank you for the flowers you sent to the hospital," Tristan said, slightly uncomfortable with making such major moves without him. "He spoke highly of you after the last deal which is why I came back."

"Is that the only reason?" Bambi asked. "I'd think it would be because supply's low."

He smiled feeling dumb. "That too."

Bambi observed him deeper. "Why are you walking through *this* door?"

"Ma'am?"

She smiled. "I'd prefer Mrs. Kennedy."

"Sorry, Mrs. Kennedy." He cleared his throat and was realizing quickly just how much he was out of his league. "What door do you mean?"

"You're in the middle of it all right now." She pointed at him. "You're at the point where things can go either way. One road leads to darkness like you'd never imagine. The other goes back to the things you know like family and a peace of mind. Are you sure you want to proceed?"

"I don't understand."

"I think you do."

He swallowed. "Mrs. Kennedy, I was born a slave. For years I had to clean up for a wealthy white family with only a few hours a night of sleep. I hated my life and everything about it and then I met Kennard. He took me in without judging and all I want to do is keep things going for him. Until he gets better." he exhaled. "I know you said I'm at the crossroad where I can go either way but with all due respect I'm already down the dark path. And if you don't mind, I'd like to proceed."

Bambi nodded and looked at Race who was holding the duffle full of paper he just handed them.

"It looks good," Race said.

Bambi sighed because her heart told her to kick his young ass out of her shop. After all, she was a mother and he was someone's son. But she knew well enough that young men did what they willed and there was nothing she could do to change it. Best he deal with her than someone else with ugly ulterior motives.

"My partner says the money looks good." She nodded to a man who walked to the back and returned with coke in a brown duffle. "Welcome to the dark side, Tristan. I hope you ready for hell."

Gasper was bent over the back of the couch in the trap house while Tristan was fucking him from behind. Their relationship worked because Gasper didn't talk about what they did when they were out in the world. It was almost like it didn't happen. They realized the need for both of them to hide their sexuality and so they remained mums.

Tristan was just about to reach an orgasm when the front door opened. His jaw dropped when he saw who was standing in front of him.

His brother, Clayton.

He didn't even know he knew the address but he'd followed him and Kennard one day.

"Oh my, Gawd!" Clayton pointed as Tristan and Gasper pulled up their pants. "What the fuck is going on in here?"

Tristan felt faint as he tried to process the scene. "We were just fucking around, man," Tristan laughed. "Wrestling and stuff because he play too much."

"Nigga, I just saw you plunging into a dude. And I'm gonna tell, ma and Kennard when he wakes up." He pointed. "As a matter of fact I'm gonna tell everybody about this shit." He laughed harder. "I know Kennard gonna be mad he left you in charge when he wake up. Wait until the nigga find out."

Gasper paced the floor. He felt this was a family matter that didn't require his attention. "Tristan, I'd love to stay but I gotta bounce."

Gasper moved to the door just as Tristan pulled his gun and shot him in the back of the head. Clayton leapt backwards and covered his mouth. "What did you just do?" he yelled looking down at Gasper's corpse. "Why you kill him?"

Tristan murdered him because he couldn't let him roam the world with Clayton knowing he had sex with him.

In frenzy, Tristan paced the floor with tears rolling down his face. Next to Kennard walking in on him this was the worst-case scenario. "You shouldn't have come here, Clayton." He wiped his tears away with the back of his burnt hand that still held the gun. "Why the fuck are you here?" He pointed at him with the barrel.

Clayton was too stunned to move. "I...I was...you know...wanted to see if you needed help. Since Kennard is in the hospital. Then I was about to pick up the girls."

"But I told you not to come here! I told you I could handle it so why are you here?"

Clayton was so scared he froze in place. This mad man was not his young brother. This person was a killer. All this time he thought Tristan was a push over and now he was learning the hard way that he was anything but. "I just wanted to help. That's all."

Tristan pointed the gun at him. "You're going to tell ma and Kennard and I can't have that."

"I was just playing," Clayton said with his hands in the air. "I won't tell anybody. I promise."

"I don't believe you and I wish I could." He wiped tears away again and aimed at Clayton causing him to duck. "I may have to kill you." He walked up to him. "Get on your knees."

"Tristan, please—"

"Get on your fucking knees."

Clayton dropped down and raised his hands higher. "Tristan, I don't want to die in here. Not like this."

Tristan thought hard about every evil thing he did to him as a kid. He remembered how he tormented him and treated him like anything but a brother. He even recalled Fashna and all the nights he tormented her knowing what their sister went through.

"You want to live?" Tristan asked breathing heavily.

"More than anything."

Tristan released his zipper while still crying and removed his penis. "Then suck it."

Clayton's eyes widened. "Tristan...you can't be serious I—"

"Suck it or die, nigga!" Tristan was limp. Nothing about it turned him on but he knew if he forced him they'd both have secrets.

"Tristan...I...I..."

Tristan pressed the barrel of his weapon on the top of his head. He would shoot him and not hesitate one bit. The only reason he was still alive was because of his mother. No matter how much he hated him he knew Zoe couldn't take another child dying. Especially with Kennard being in the hospital.

Clayton gazed across the room at Gasper's body, opened his mouth and did what was demanded. He tasted Gaspers feces and blood and wanted to throw up.

All the while a part of him died.

CHAPTER THIRTY-SIX

SERWA

"Now We Fight"

Serwa and Lumo were speaking secretly in the back of the shop. The security guard returned and ate his meal in the front of the television, unaware that Fashna was missing.

"I will never forgive her," Serwa whispered. "She left us." She pointed at the floor. "Didn't even bother to take us with her. When we would've taken our chance long ago if we hadn't waited on her when she was sick." Serwa paused to take a breath because the anger was consuming. "Look what happened to me." She opened her mouth. "Look at my broken teeth, from where Clayton kicked me."

Lumo looked back at the guard to make sure he wasn't staring at them. "I know what happened to you was wrong and Zoe will get what she deserves. I'll see to it." She paused. "But don't be angry with Fashna, Serwa. Be proud. She finally got the courage to do what we always wanted. To fight."

"But what about us? When Clayton comes back and realizes Fashna is gone they'll probably kill us. Thinking that we'll run next. We have lost our chance, friend."

"That's what I wanted to talk to you about. I have good news." Lumo smiled. "One of my clients today was a friend of Maganda, Issa and Ori."

Serwa's eyes widened. "You heard word from them?"

"Lower your voice," Lumo said looking at the guard who was still eating.

"How did this happen?" Serwa moved closer.

"Like I said, one of my clients is friends with them and she needed us to know that if we wanted to escape she had someone who could help us. But she suggested we move as soon as possible."

"So they're still here? In America?"

"Yes, my friend."

Serwa hugged Lumo and separated quickly. "This is great news."

"I know but what do we do?"

"I have a plan," Serwa said looking at the security guard. "A really good one."

Serwa and Lumo had Quentin, the security guard, in the bathroom giving him a treat of all treats. Serwa was on her knees sucking his dick while Lumo licked his nipples like he requested. One minute he was told that Serwa had a seizure on the bathroom floor and the next he was being seduced by two beautiful women.

He knew it was a ploy to seek his help to escape and he had a surprise when they were done.

As they continued to work Quentin could feel himself reaching an orgasm and when he did he exploded in Serwa's mouth. His clumpy semen streamed down her throat. The moment he was satisfied he pushed her away, pulled his pants up and glared at them both. "That was great but I'm not helping you leave." He pointed down at Serwa. "So forget about it."

Serwa sighed. “Please, they beat us and—”

“Whatever they do to you is none of my business.” He pointed at himself. “They’re my employers and I could give a fuck about either of you black bitches.” He paused. “And if you tell anybody about this I will make both of your lives a living hell.” He pulled the door opened and rushed out.

The black men of America were disappointing her. They seemed to not care about their women and their hearts were heavy.

Upset, Lumo looked at her and sighed. “Now what?”

Serwa winked and focused on her hand. When Lumo followed her gaze she saw she was holding his gun.

“Now we fight!”

Serwa and Lumo just finished tying Tano up in the basement at the house. Clayton was upstairs moping around. He was so distraught the security guard dropped them off and his truck remained at the shop. They figured his depression was about Fashna missing although Serwa sensed there was more.

When Tano's mouth was gagged and her arms tied using ripped shirts Serwa, Lumo and Kessie talked in the corner about the plan. "When Clayton comes downstairs we rush his ass and shoot him in the gut."

"I say you shoot him the moment you see his face," Lumo warned. "We don't want him to overpower you and take the gun."

"I promise you, Lumo, he may do many things but he won't take this gun." She was so passionate she trembled with anger.

When Clayton opened the door, the moment his foot hit the last step Serwa slid across the floor and unleashed. She never fired a gun before that moment but she was a quick study.

Zoe sat in her car outside of her house she was on hold waiting to speak to the hospital about Kennard's status. He was doing badly earlier and they weren't sure if he was going to make it.

"Hello, this is Zoe Xavier." She pressed the phone to her ear. "I'm calling about Kennard Black."

"One minute." She could hear the woman typing on the keyboard in the background. "Okay, yes, I see. We need to know what you want done with the body."

"His body?"

"Yes, would you like it moved to a funeral home?" she asked sarcastically.

Suddenly Zoe could barely breathe. "He's...he's dead?"

"Yes, you're calling for Kennard Black right?"

"I am."

"Well he's *been* dead." The nurse was tactless. "Now what do you want done with his remains?"

Zoe hung up, gripped the steering wheel and vomited in her lap. The car smelled like blue cheese. Her entire world was rocked with the news and she felt dizzy. Where was she going to go now that he was dead? What was she going to do?

She was just about to call Clayton for help since she didn't see his truck when her phone rang. She answered although her thoughts were still entrenched in deliria. "Hel…hello." She wiped the tears from her face.

"Is this Zoe Xavier?"

"Yes," she sighed.

"This is detective Ramsey and I need to schedule a home visit. We received information that you're housing undocumented workers in your home. Is this true?"

Zoe ended the call and pushed open the door and ran inside the house. Having no idea that Fashna placed the call to help.

Serwa, Lumo and Kessie were on their way out of the house after stealing Clayton's keys when they saw Zoe coming inside from the window. "Let's hide in the kitchen," Kessie said. "Quick."

“Fuck this bitch,” Serwa said clutching the gun in her palm. “I’m not hiding anymore.”

They were about to walk up to her when Zoe rushed upstairs leaving the door wide open. She was so shaken up that she didn’t see them on the left of her in the hallway. Serwa was about to follow and put a bullet in the back of her head when Lumo stopped her. “It’s not necessary, friend. Let’s go.”

“But she deserves to pay for everything she did to us.”

Lumo grabbed her arm so hard it hurt. “We are free, Serwa.” Spit flew from her mouth as she spoke with passion. “You follow her and you suffer her same fate. Look at her life, Serwa. Look at how she changed. She’s miserable. Her man isn’t here and she doesn’t have her beauty anymore. She has already received her karma and I have no doubt more is coming. Let’s leave and find Maganda. Let’s start our lives. Please.”

Warm tears rolled down Serwa’s face as she considered Lumo’s wise words. She looked at the steps once more and ran away with Lumo and Kessie.”

In tears, Zoe poured lighting fluid everywhere but downstairs in the basement. She didn't bother to see if the girls were there because she wanted to burn any evidence of having slaves.

Including their bodies.

When the upstairs was speckled with fluid she stood at the front door and lit a match, tossing it down. Like flame on dynamite it rolled through the house burning everything near.

Seeing the furniture ignite she gazed at what was left of her life. She'd come so far and now it would end like this and she wondered if she didn't deserve this fate. She had a responsibility to be better to those she had power over. Instead of honoring this power she abused it and became a monster.

Sobbing uncontrollably she walked out the door, having no clue that Clayton's body was in the basement along with Tano who was still alive.

She was almost to the car when suddenly a black luxury sedan with tinted windows pulled in front of her, blocking her path. The back window rolled down and Zoe was stunned at who she was looking at. “Mrs. Xavier? How did you know where I lived?”

“I told you to beware and you didn’t listen. So I’m here to make you pay.”

A male driver emerged from the car and aimed a gun at Zoe. Before she could run he fired at her, the bullet penetrating the flesh of her neck. When the deed was done she fled away from the scene leaving Zoe wet on the street soaked in her own blood.

EPILOGUE

Zoe and Clayton's funeral went down without a hitch. The only attendees were Tristan and Woody. Tristan sat in the truck with Woody, sharing a bottle of Hennessey. They were still at the graveyard and night was approaching.

When he went by the house to talk to his mother he was shocked when he saw her in the street. Luckily he had a soldier with him who was able to drive them to the hospital where Zoe eventually died.

"You think we can do this shit? Alone?" Woody asked.

Tristan sighed. "I don't see why not." He shrugged. "We have the men and the connection with the Kennedy's. It looks like we're in the best position to keep the work moving if you ask me."

Woody looked out the window at the gravesite. "Niggas gonna try us because we young." He sighed. "They never gonna let us be in the beginning."

"Then we have to teach them a lesson they will remember." Tristan paused. "Man, I just buried my mother and brother. Plus Kennard coming home in a week. I want things set up for him and if anybody stands in the way of that I'm willing to deal with them. I don't want him worrying about how we gonna eat. He's talking and moving around but it's gonna be at least a year before he's back to normal. My only question is if you're with me or not?"

"You know I am." He tossed some Hennessey down his throat. "I still can't believe people thought Kennard was dead though. Niggas walking up to me asking me if I was straight." He shook his head. "Creepy shit."

"Yeah, apparently a nigga with the same name was murdered and died in that same hospital. From what I hear he'd been in there for weeks but nobody claimed his body. I heard they ended up cremating his ass."

"What you gonna do 'bout Gina? You gonna let her get away with what she did to him?"

"When Kennard woke up the first thing he said was let him handle it. I think he got plans for her I'm gonna let him own." He paused. "But I don't want to rehash all that shit right now,

Woody. I just wanna move on and get things ready for Kennard."

"You got it, I already said."

"How things with you and Fashna though?"

"She good but I think she misses them girls." He paused. "Sometimes I think she blames me for not helping them too and other times I think she blames herself."

"I know...but at least she got you now."

Woody nodded. "Yeah but I don't know if its enough." He sighed. "Is there anything you need from me?"

Tristan looked ahead at the moon, which was tipping out from the purple sky. "Actually, Woody, there is..."

Woody and Tristan were at Tristan's new house that he rented for Kennard. It was bigger than the last crib with a rent to own option in case they liked it enough to buy. Kennard was returning in one day and things were running smoothly.

Tristan placed two beers on the table and turned on the TV, which was already on the national news.

"Oh shit, Tristan, this is it," Woody said raising the sound.

Authorities are still asking the public for information about a break in that left an entire family murdered. The victims were 62-year-old Edward Xavier and 57-year-old Violet Xavier.

Authorities say a 911 call was placed just before 11 o'clock on Friday night reporting gunfire and screams in the Texas Estate. Police say after the crime, the two suspects ransacked the house and removed jewelry and cash.

The crime is believed to be related to a human trafficking ring that the victims were involved in although this has not been verified.

Both suspects were wearing black hoodies, blue latex gloves and had their faces covered with a black bandana, according to law enforcement. Surveillance video shows the suspects approaching on foot but they believe a vehicle was waiting further away from the property.

And elderly woman, Celeste Xavier, who appears to be one of the workers, was later questioned but has refused to speak on the issue.

Anyone with information regarding this crime is asked to contact the Texas Rangers.

Woody turned the sound down and looked at Tristan. This was their work and it was perfect. After the funeral they drove back to Texas and successfully pulled off the crime so that Tristan could get the revenge for his mother's death and for them ruining their lives. He learned that Mrs. Xavier was responsible and was dead set on making her pay.

He also dropped off some money to Celeste and told her to go on with her life and that he wished her well. She hugged him and left the scene.

"You good now?" Woody asked with a sly smile.

Tristan nodded. "I'm satisfied." He responded and gave him dap.

ONE YEAR LATER

Fashna was in the mall buying jeans because she was five months pregnant with Woody's baby and nothing seemed to fit. Life was good with her husband and she thanked God everyday. He treated her right and she felt protected in their home.

Still, she was lonely.

She was on her way out when she looked across the parking lot and saw her cousin Maganda along with Issa, Ori, Serwa, Lumo and Kessie approaching the mall. They were laughing happily together and her body heated up with love.

Ever since Fashna left without helping them she was consumed with guilt. First she talked them into coming to this country under false dreams and then she abandoned them to save herself. The thing was she had no idea that Woody would rescue her that night and she had to take the offer.

But did she make a mistake?

In her dreams they hated her and she hoped it wasn't true.

When Maganda saw Fashna she pressed her hands against her lips and cried into her fingers. Unable to control the love rushing through her body she ran past the cars and toward Fashna and gripped her lovingly. "Cousin, you, you're beautiful," Maganda cried. She grabbed her face and looked into her eyes. "Oh how I missed you, cousin," she continued in her native language. "Oh how I missed you."

The other girls were excited and hugged her also but not everyone was so pleased. "I'll wait in the car," Serwa said angrily.

"Serwa, I—" Fashna screamed.

It was too late she already walked away.

Tears rolled down Fashna's face because she understood Serwa's pain but it didn't make her feel any better. "After all this time, she still hates me," Fashna whispered. "I prayed that God would talk to her heart for me. Guess it didn't work."

"Serwa will come around, cousin," Maganda touched her face while Lumo grabbed one hand and Kessie the other. Issa and Ori stood in front of her smiling. "So how are you? Because you look amazing."

"Well I'm married to Woody." She touched her bulging belly and tried to cheer up. "And I'm having his baby. A little boy."

"Great news." Lumo said excitedly. "Woody went after what he wanted. That's admirable."

"Thank you...but where are you guys living?" She looked at all of them. "Because you all look so beautiful. Like models."

It was true, their hair was impeccable and they all wore designer clothing and carried expensive purses on their arm.

But why were they silent after hearing her question?

"Well...are you guys married too?" Fashna asked.

"I'm dating but the others are focused on the business," Maganda said her voice tainted with slight guilt.

"What business?" She frowned.

"I don't want to say much, let's just say we work for a very powerful woman," Maganda continued. "Who has allowed us all to live in her home as long as we handle our business."

Lumo's chin rose and Fashna knew whatever they were doing was gunplay related.

"Well, what's her name?" Fashna asked excitedly.

"Nine Prophet," Lumo said proudly. "Of the Prophet family."

CARTEL PUBLICATIONS
PRESENTS
RED
BONE
Red Bone 3
THE RISE OF THE FOLD
T. STYLES
NATIONAL BESTSELLING AUTHOR OF RAUNCHY

The Cartel Publications Order Form

www.thecartelpublications.com

Inmates **ONLY** receive novels for $10.00 per book.

(Mail Order **MUST** come from inmate directly to receive discount)

Title	Qty	Price
Shyt List 1	________	$15.00
Shyt List 2	________	$15.00
Shyt List 3	________	$15.00
Shyt List 4	________	$15.00
Shyt List 5	________	$15.00
Pitbulls In A Skirt	________	$15.00
Pitbulls In A Skirt 2	________	$15.00
Pitbulls In A Skirt 3	________	$15.00
Pitbulls In A Skirt 4	________	$15.00
Victoria's Secret	________	$15.00
Poison 1	________	$15.00
Poison 2	________	$15.00
Hell Razor Honeys	________	$15.00
Hell Razor Honeys 2	________	$15.00
A Hustler's Son	________	$15.00
A Hustler's Son 2	________	$15.00
Black and Ugly	________	$15.00
Black and Ugly As Ever	________	$15.00
Year Of The Crackmom	________	$15.00
Deadheads	________	$15.00
The Face That Launched A Thousand Bullets	________	$15.00
The Unusual Suspects	________	$15.00
Miss Wayne & The Queens of DC	________	$15.00
Paid In Blood (eBook Only)	________	$15.00
Raunchy	________	$15.00
Raunchy 2	________	$15.00
Raunchy 3	________	$15.00
Mad Maxxx	________	$15.00
Quita's Dayscare Center	________	$15.00
Quita's Dayscare Center 2	________	$15.00
Pretty Kings	________	$15.00
Pretty Kings 2	________	$15.00
Pretty Kings 3	________	$15.00
Silence Of The Nine	________	$15.00
Silence Of The Nine 2	________	$15.00
Prison Throne	________	$15.00
Drunk & Hot Girls	________	$15.00

Hersband Material	________	$15.00
The End: How To Write A Bestselling Novel In 30 Days (Non-Fiction Guide)	________	$15.00
Upscale Kittens	________	$15.00
Wake & Bake Boys	________	$15.00
Young & Dumb	________	$15.00
Young & Dumb 2:	________	$15.00
Tranny 911	________	$15.00
Tranny 911: Dixie's Rise	________	$15.00
First Comes Love, Then Comes Murder	________	$15.00
Luxury Tax	________	$15.00
The Lying King	________	$15.00
Crazy Kind Of Love	________	$15.00
And They Call Me God	________	$15.00
The Ungrateful Bastards	________	$15.00
Lipstick Dom	________	$15.00
A School of Dolls	________	$15.00
Hoetic Justice	________	$15.00
KALI: Raunchy Relived	________	$15.00
Skeezers	________	$15.00
You Kissed Me, Now I Own You	________	$15.00
Nefarious	________	$15.00

Please add $5.00 **PER BOOK** for shipping and handling.

The Cartel Publications * P.O. BOX 486 OWINGS MILLS MD 21117

Name: ________________

Address: ________________

City/State: ________________

Contact/Email: ________________

Please allow 5-7 BUSINESS days before shipping.

The Cartel Publications is NOT responsible for prison orders rejected.

NO PERSONAL CHECKS ACCEPTED

STAMPS NO LONGER ACCEPTED

CPSIA information can be obtained
at www.ICGtesting.com
Printed in the USA
LVOW12s1455060516
487046LV00001B/205/P